THE DSA SEASON ONE, BOOK ONE

THE *CLEARING*

Also by Lou Paduano

The Greystone Saga

Signs of Portents
Tales from Portents
The Medusa Coin
Pathways in the Dark
A Circle of Shadows

Greystone-in-Training

Hammer and Anvil

THE DSA SEASON ONE, BOOK ONE

THE CLEARING

Lou Paduano

Eleven Ten Publishing LLC

GRAND ISLAND, NEW YORK

Eleven Ten Publishing LLC
282 Fareway Lane
Grand Island, NY 14072

Publisher's note: This is a work of fiction. Names, characters, places, and incidents either are the product of the author's imagination or are used fictitiously. Any resemblance to actual events, locales, or persons, living or dead, is entirely coincidental.

Printed in the United States of America
Edited by JD Book Services.
Cover art design by MiblArt

First edition published 2019

Library of Congress Cataloguing in Publication Data
Paduano, Lou
The Clearing / Lou Paduano

LCCN: 2019914242
ISBN-13: 978-1-944965-17-4 (paperback)
ISBN-13: 978-1-944965-15-0 (eBook)

CHAPTER ONE

He hated the job.

"10-43. Officer in pursuit."

It was his father's dream, his father's wishes that had pushed him to go through the academy, to display the shield proudly on his chest. It was never him, never Ben Riley's purpose or aspiration.

That night was exactly the reason why.

The night's patrol ran routine. There were no great explosions of violence, no upheavals of murder and chaos. It had been a simple patrol through the Lovejoy District of Buffalo with his partner behind the wheel. He'd offered to drive and was shot down — the start of every shift shared; an eternal joke to lighten the mood.

"I repeat, officer in pursuit." Emily's voice blasted in his ear as she fed directions for support to follow in pursuit of the suspect.

A laughable term. 'Suspect.' They'd pulled over the mid-size sedan on Walden just outside the park. It was a routine traffic violation and nothing more. The right taillight was out. Ben retrieved his citation pad, hand at the door, when the gentleman inside — lanky and young — made a run for it.

Ben went after him. No hesitation. No regret. Just doing his job, exactly the way his father would have wanted.

"They're cutting through the park."

Emily stayed behind to take a closer look at the abandoned vehicle. No words were shared between them, and none were necessary. Partners for almost his entire career, their movements were intuitive, practiced and measured. He'd never known anyone like Sergeant Emily Wright, whose very presence made the job palatable, able to hold his interest and sustain his hope.

Police work meant witnessing the darkness of humanity—attempting to hold the line against a world of sin and despair while somehow carving a small piece of a life out for oneself. The job took its toll, wearing at him, threatening to squeeze joy from his very vocabulary. But Ben kept pushing forward, working it out a little every day. He did it for his father, for Emily, and for everyone else.

Music filtered through the air; the park disappeared behind them. A fence hop and they raced down Wex Avenue, cutting west into the residential area. Single-family homes ran the block. Windows were open even with the rain beating along the ground, the long winter finally over. The rhythm matched both Ben's pounding heart and the slapping of his shoes against the slick pavement.

He closed in on the man, fingers outstretched. Warnings passed from his lips. *Stop. Halt. Freeze.* All were ignored or lost in the wind. His hand grazed the man's jacket before swiping nothing but air. Stumbling forward from the failed attempt, Ben plowed into the side of a parked car. The man ducked to the right to avoid the collision.

Three doors down, the rain at his back, the shadowed suspect leapt over the short, metal fence of the property and blitzed for the porch. Ben followed, unclasping the lock on his holster. He kept the weapon at his side, refusing to allow things to escalate further. He jumped the fence, eyes never wavering from the man at the front door.

The figure didn't reach for keys to enter the domicile. Instead, a keypad beamed to the right; drilled into the cracked and warped siding. The electronic display demanded a code, which was quickly punched in with the aid of a small scrap of paper tucked between his fingers. Five clicks and the front door released from the frame. The man slipped into the shadows of the home.

Before the door could close, a hair's breadth from shutting him out, Ben caught it. He hesitated for only a second, then pulled at his radio.

"243 Wex, Em," he announced. "I'm heading inside."

"Ben, don't!" she shouted through the static. "Wait for—"

The door closed behind him and the radio fell silent. Darkness filled the room. Ben shuffled his feet forward slowly, a hand over his father's Ruger. The sound of metal clanged under his step. Confused, the determined officer took a second step and then a third.

Lights came alive overhead. Ben's eyes widened. For his entire life, Ben had sought something bigger, a purpose and an answer for his life, never truly believing he would ever find one.

Until now.

There was no home before him, no living room or kitchen, and no early-twentieth-century decor repaired a dozen times over during the decades. The home wasn't a home at all, but a vast warehouse extending as far as he could see. Compartments lined the walls, and there were workstations in the center. Lab equipment sat in each, chemicals filtering through beakers in some and high-tech medical assemblies positioned in others. Machine arms from an assembly line manufactured devices that the overwhelmed officer failed to recognize. It was technology unlike any seen in the open market. Computer terminals and interfaces adorned every surface in the space, displaying data readouts, formulas, and code—all of which went over Ben's head.

At the heart of the operation was a cityscape. It was a scale model, but of no metropolis the young officer had seen before. Walls confined the facsimile, the word UTOPIA emblazoned along the base. Ben shifted for a closer look when he noticed the floor beneath him change from solid to scattered.

The grating allowed him to scan below his current position. No longer at ground level, he was suspended many times higher from the bottom of the structure. His feet stumbled from the jarring loss of all sense of direction. Hands grabbed for stability, and he caught a protective railing at the last moment before falling.

"Where the hell am I?" he struggled to ask. "Where—?"

His suspect was gone. The object of his pursuit and the reason he'd stepped foot into the home in the first place. Where once there might have been a dozen places to hide, innumerable shadows existed in the warehouse.

Ben took a step forward then stopped. A sound buzzed in his ear, holding him in place. It started like a bee along his collar and he quickly took a step back. The sound grew with each step.

His radio was back and Emily's voice called to him from out-side. The clarity sharpened the moment he turned around and caught sight of the entrance.

The door returned—white as ever with cracked paint and gaps at the bottom of the frame. It was an anomaly compared with the rest of the place. Ben returned to the door and opened it.

Emily Wright raised her sidearm and Ben threw up his hands, smiling at her arrival.

"Em," he said as he inched away from the frame. "You have to see—"

A hand slammed into his back, shoving him toward the stairs. Ben stumbled across the porch. He caught the railing be-fore tripping down the landing. He spun around, but it was too late. The door shut, crashing into the frame with finality.

"Ben," Emily said. "Are you all right?"

"I'm fine," he replied, eyes locked on the door. "But you won't believe what's in there. It's—"

Flashing lights washed over them and tires screeched to a halt on the street. Their support arrived: a pair of officers exiting the vehicle to join them.

"Everything all right?"

Emily nodded, a hand raised to hold them back. "We're fine."

Ben pulled her back toward the door. "Em, you have to see this."

He reached for the knob and twisted. It failed to budge. Ben pushed with his left while doing the same motion, all to no avail. Perplexed, he turned to the panel along the siding.

"Ben," Emily started, confusion resting in her eyes. "Leave it. The guy's car was clean. No idea why he bothered to bolt. We can have a forensics team take a look and—"

"Let me try."

"How are you going to pick the right combination?" she asked. "There must be thousands."

Ben agreed. Five numbers in the sequence meant the chance of stumbling upon the correct iteration was infinitesimal. Still, he pressed on. Covering his finger with his sleeve, Ben carefully tapped a string of numbers, then stepped back.

The door groaned open from the frame.

He smiled, hands spread wide in the air. "Magic."

"Please," she scoffed.

"Say it with me," he continued. "Magic."

She shook her head as she stepped into the home. "I'm not saying it."

Ben followed, waiting for an exclamation from his partner to fill the warehouse. Only no cry rose from Emily, and no warehouse spread before them.

He entered the home to find the buzzing overhead light of a shallow hallway. The living room to the right held water-damaged wood for flooring and battered furniture in desperate need of repair. Peeling paint—yellow or what could have been yellow at some earlier date—streamed up the stairs to the second floor.

No cityscape model. No technology leagues beyond anything they had ever seen. No wonder. No amazement of any kind.

"This is what you wanted to show me?"

Ben turned around and the door was still in place. He stepped out then back in, the results never changing. "Not even close."

All that remained for Ben Riley were questions—unceasing mysteries that would haunt him for the rest of his days.

CHAPTER TWO

It fell apart in twenty-two minutes.

One week was spent on planning, research, and back-tracing — all to figure out the target and the proper strategy to take care of the job. Three days spent going over the breach angle, the layout of the building. Hours spent poring over every minute detail, repeated until each player in the drama could recite the priority of every other person both in the field and at Bethesda One.

It all fell apart in the end.

Susan Metcalf was standing in the hall of the subbasement when the call came in. It didn't arrive through her personal cell, which rested in her hand. She had spent the previous hour reassuring her superiors — not quite how *she* viewed them — of their control over the situation and convincing them that it would be handled before the close of business. It was not a promise — it was a guarantee made on the trust she placed in her team. They were the four people most qualified out of any government agency to track down the suspect and apprehend him.

Oliver Blake. She preferred 'the suspect.' The term made him sound as inhuman as his actions. One week earlier he had released a contagion on an unsuspecting cafe in Spokane, Washington. Twenty-three people had died beside their beverages — men, women, and children — the strain was indiscriminate in its final judgment. Twenty-three bodies on the floor while one man walked away, satisfied at the result.

Every agency had been brought to task. Every organization shifted their top priority to include the maniac in the gas mask who had terrorized a simple coffee shop for kicks. The Department of Special Assignments, designated DSA, trailed the surveillance image of the figure to the man himself and nailed down a name.

Oliver Blake.

They took the lead, Metcalf coordinating with the CDC and Homeland Security every step of the way. This wasn't about ownership or jurisdiction. This was about justice for those fallen. The field team had breached Blake's laboratory at 0738 hours.

Twenty-two minutes ago — a lifetime for her.

"Director?"

Zac Modine, the Head of Operational Support and Research, peered out the door to the Operations hub with a headset in his hand. The heavyset tech's gaze dropped toward the ground rather than meet her full on.

"What happened?"

"It's the team."

With her phone tucked away, Metcalf entered the room. Immediately, the sound of a dozen individuals working in tandem filled her senses. Typing away, analysts sought solutions to problems yet to be determined. They were organizing detailed reports of their findings — precautionary measures to take if action was needed.

The back wall of the extensive space monitored the current operation in detail. To the right were bio-readings of the field team. Four images of each member of the team occupied the screens. The displays filtered through their vital signs, including heart rates and synaptic activity. To the left was a layout of Blake's compound: an abandoned home on the outskirts of Deer Park.

The center console displayed an inside look at the team's progress. Only, it no longer showed the home or the equipment found within. The bodycam had been positioned to show the team itself. Three figures filled the view, half-mask respirators still in place for containment protocol.

Metcalf slipped on her headset and angry voices immediately flooded her ears.

"You don't know what—"

"I'm not going to argue about this any—"

"We need to—"

"Enough!" Metcalf yelled through the communication line.

"What happened?"

Ruth Heller stepped forward on the display, the other two falling silent. Heller wore military fatigue pants. She held a scanner with one hand while the other pushed short strawberry-blond locks behind her ear. "Blake's dead," she huffed, the sound crystal clear with the comm inside the gas mask.

Their objective was twofold—find the man and his research. Both goals were necessary to the success of the mission. Taking the man dead or alive had never been a sticking point.

"I don't see why—"

"There was something in the lab next to where we found him," she said over the director. Metcalf noticed the operations crew creeping closer to the monitors to listen. "Specimens. Samples. I don't know exactly."

"The toxin from the cafe?"

"It was locked down. We thought it was, but..." She trailed off, struggling to find the words.

Metcalf held firm to the headset. "Agent Heller? Has there been a breach?"

"No breach," Ruth said, shaking her head. "Negative on breach. Samples have been contained."

"Then what is it? Your gear?"

The black man to her left cut her off. He carried a Glock in a shoulder holster and an M-16 at his side. The consummate soldier, Lincoln MacKenzie was always prepared for war. "Our gear isn't the issue."

"Then what is?"

"Grissom," Ruth said. "He's—"

"He's down," Lincoln finished, fingers tight to his weapon.

"Agent Heller?" Metcalf called. Her heart pounded, the noise of the Operations room deafening. It swallowed her thoughts, threatened to spin her out of control. Jacob Grissom ran the field team. As the Deputy Director of the DSA, Grissom had helped her form the department from the ground up. He had been by her side for the better part of a decade. He brought purpose and direction to everything they did, every struggle and every victory. "We are still reading Agent Grissom's bio-signs on our end. They're cutting in and out like the rest of yours due to interference in the lab, but they're still there."

"I told you!" the third figure on the monitor snapped. Morgan Dunleavy stood taller than the pair, towering in the room with flawless ebony skin and deep brown eyes. "We never should have left him in there."

Ruth seethed, "I'm done talking about this with you, Morgan. So back off or I swear to—"

"Knock it off," Metcalf hissed into the line.

"He was infected. The specimen activated when he came into contact with it, and the pathogen was released."

"But his mask?"

Heller shook her head. "Direct contact negated our protocols. The virus was in his bloodstream before we had a chance to react. The only reason we're still standing is because of Grissom."

Metcalf covered up the receiver on her set, then turned to Zac. "I need the op rundown. Now."

It was in her hand in the next breath. She glanced through it, noting every milestone. The breach occurred at 0738 hours to the southern wall of the structure. The team split upon entry. Ruth and Lincoln focused on the server room and the research of Oliver Blake. Grissom and Morgan attempted to locate the man himself.

At 0751, Ruth had checked in. The servers had been wiped clean. It was a definite surprise, considering they represented the man's entire life. It was research maintained in secret for years from what they'd learned in their own study of the situation. Blake would never delete something so vital to his being.

That summed up the next line item with a nice question mark as well. Grissom and Morgan had located Oliver Blake in the hall, dead, at 0754. The gun sat in his hand, the initial thought suicide.

Metcalf skimmed the rest. Nothing indicated chatter of a secondary objective. Nothing mentioned Grissom leaving behind his partner and his duty to pursue an unspoken mission.

"Why was he in the lab?" she asked, more to herself than those around her, but the team sought to fill the void of her silence.

"He was right next to me," Morgan said. "We found Blake and were examining the wound. Evidence pointed to self-infliction, but I wanted to run some tests on the gun. When I looked up, Grissom was down the hall in the lab looking through the samples inside."

"One fell. He went to catch it and —" Ruth couldn't finish.

"He sealed the lab," Lincoln said.

"Grissom saved us," Morgan continued. "Now we should save him."

"Don't," Ruth snapped. "Just don't. You saw him. You saw what one minute of exposure did to Grissom. You want that out in the world?"

"No. I want *him* out in the world. And we can save him without risk to ourselves — without direct contact. I have to try."

"No," Metcalf said. "We don't know what he's been exposed to. We have no way of handling the toxin."

"He's dying in there!"

"Metcalf," Lincoln uttered, the name straining from his lips. He pulled the Glock from his right shoulder. "Let me do this. He doesn't deserve to suffer."

"Put that damn gun away, Lincoln!" Morgan shouted. "Before I shove it up your —"

"You're going to expose us to the same —"

Their voices bellowed through the line. They echoed in the Operations hub. Tears fell from the cheeks of the analysts behind Metcalf. Sorrow filled the faces of everyone in attendance. The fighting was not that of professionals, but of colleagues and friends. Family, of a sort: one built through years of training and experience with the man locked in a room down the hall.

"We have no way of knowing what this is," Metcalf started, silencing the trio on the screen. It should have been a flawless operation, the same as Grissom had executed since the department's inception. "We have no idea what Blake was working on, especially since his servers have been wiped clean. We also don't know whether he was aware of our arrival or some other player intervened. We don't know anything."

"We have to try," Morgan said. Her medical training shone through in every situation. Her time as a physician dictated her priorities.

"He's already gone, Morgan," Lincoln answered. "At least my way —"

And they were lost to it again: their failure and their anger. Ruth, however, maintained a modicum of respect, head bowed in thought and prayer for a moment until she tapped her mask.

"I need your orders, Director."

Metcalf understood the meaning of her statement, the truth behind the request being made. She knew it had been coming the moment the call arrived from the team before the predetermined exfil time. Ruth wanted more than to ask Metcalf's opinion. She wanted absolution from what had to be done. She wanted to put it on someone else, anyone other than the team.

That left Metcalf. It always left Metcalf.

"Director?"

Every choice fell to her. Every stare in the room waited for an answer. She became the center of the world for the DSA in that moment — but she was elsewhere. She relived a decade's worth of memories in an instant, recalling the man who had stood at her side through it all. A memorial in the blink of an eye, for that was all the time she had left.

"CDC agents are en route," Metcalf said, her words cold and booming in the silence of the operations hub. "Lock down the structure then proceed to exfil point C."

"Grissom will die," Morgan replied. Her eyes pleaded for more. The bio-readings flickered and faded. Grissom's heart rate had slowed, and then it finally flatlined with the rest of his readings. "Grissom is dying in there!"

"Metcalf, this isn't right," Lincoln agreed. "He deserves a quick end."

Ruth said nothing. The mantle of leadership already caused her shoulders to slump forward.

"Follow my orders," the director commanded. Disdain shot her way. It surrounded her in the faces of everyone in the room. Zac, especially, looked shocked and unable to stand at her side as the words echoed through the line. "Extraction in one hour."

"I can save him," Morgan begged. "Let me —"

"He's dead, Agent Dunleavy. Casualty of war." Metcalf removed the headset, unwilling to listen to another word. She nodded to the team, all slipping back into place to continue their work. Zac's thin glare burned through her, but eventually he returned to the monitor — plotting the course for their exfil point.

The silence abated and a dull hum filled the room. The murmurs began, the questions rising from everyone's lips. Grissom was dead and Metcalf had ordered it.

She didn't care at that moment. She couldn't care about Zac's anger or the concerns from the field team. Or about the twenty eyes that followed her departure from the Operations hub to the quiet of the hall.

CHAPTER THREE

People swarmed the E-District Precinct. The masses took control and chaos ensued. Lines formed to the right and spread the length of the lobby, barring the entrance. Ben shuffled through, his badge accepted with groans from the unfortunates left to rot due to staff budget cuts. Those officers present did what they could. They pulled support from other departments where necessary, but the damage was done. The blame was placed on the full moon hovering over the city.

It certainly took its toll on everyone, including Ben. He rubbed at his eyes, wishing for sleep on his pillow-top mattress. Nothing sounded sweeter than eight to twelve hours of rest before starting all over again.

Emily needed him, though. When she called, he didn't hear his phone. Only the missed call notification alerted him, indicating her presence at work. He found her waiting just inside, away from their shared desk. She stood at the printer, a Brooklyn Dodgers cap atop her head, short brown hair tucked tight within. The cap was a tradition, one of many held by the Wright family and passed down from her father's line for three generations—like the job itself, and their family home. The Wrights were a staple of the city, inseparable.

"Em," Ben called. He waved to grab her attention. "Hey, Emily!"

"Ben?" Her eyes connected with his, then darted around the room. She ditched the spewing papers at the printer and cut him off at the entrance. "What the hell are you doing here?"

"Is your dad all right? Are you—?"

Emily shook her head. "My dad? Ben, what are you talking

about?"

"You called me. I thought something might have happened, so I—"

"He's fine," she answered, hand to her brow. Her father's chemo treatments were starting up again. It was another attempt to save his life, each one more desperate than the last. "My dad's fine, Ben. But you shouldn't be here."

A crowd gathered in the stable, surrounding his desk in the corner. It was typical, considering the growing line outside looking for assistance. Most of the time, cops fed each other stories from the events of the day—exaggerated for laughs—all to cloud the misery and darkness seen in the city.

The job had that effect on everyone. When all you saw was the bottom, you had to reach for the top to try and find some light. That was a lesson from Ben's mother, one taught through sarcasm and laughter, one he always appreciated—and one told daily thanks to his father's impact on their home life.

When he noticed a pair of plainclothes from Homicide digging through his personal effects, Ben's gaze thinned. "What's going on?"

Emily shook her head, then grabbed his arm. She pulled him in the opposite direction, down the interrogation wing. The first room was empty. The door crashed against the paneling before swinging back. She held it open with her hand as she ushered them in for a modicum of privacy.

"Tell me you weren't there."

"Okay, I wasn't," Ben said. He leaned on the lone table in the center of the room. Emily slammed the door shut behind them. "Where wasn't I supposed to be?"

"Cut the crap, Ben."

"Your call sounded frantic and I assumed the worst," he continued, trying to calm her down. She clenched tighter and her arms crossed her chest. "Hey, talk to me."

"Did you actually listen to my message? The one where I said to stay away from the precinct?"

Ben tossed her an awkward smirk and shrugged. "I was busy, Em. I figured I'd come down and—"

"You were there again, weren't you. That damn house on Wex?" Emily let out a heated breath. Her back settled against the wall. "I asked you not to go back. I asked you to drop it."

"I can't, Em," Ben admitted. "And yeah, I was there. It's my time and I can use it however I choose."

He had gone every night for the last three weeks. He'd taken photos and circled the property for some sign of life. Nothing had cropped up since his initial visit. No visitors. No warehouse hidden inside the modest dwelling. It was just another abandoned property in the Lovejoy District as far as anyone could tell, but he'd witnessed the truth that first night: the technology, the operations, and the mystery of what was tucked beneath the surface. He was out to prove it to her — to anyone who would listen.

"I... I asked you to stop talking about it, Ben," she stammered, her words barely a whisper. No longer angry, they were filled with disappointment and sadness. "I begged you to let it go and focus on the job."

"This *is* the job, isn't it?" Her anger had dimmed, but his rose. Citations and petty crime swallowed his existence. The dregs of humanity pulled at him with each shift, but when an honest-to-God mystery presented itself, he was supposed to forget about it? The impounded car had turned up nothing in their search — the vehicle listed as stolen months earlier. The man who had run from them was a ghost. No clues. No leads. "Someone is building something in that place. Working with technology I've never seen before. No one has."

"You told me." Her gaze fell low. "Another obsession. You're always looking for more in the job, but sometimes there isn't anything more, Ben. I wish there was too, but there isn't."

"That's not what this is," he said as he pushed from the table. He reached for her, but she turned for the door. "Hey. It's not, okay? I took it up the chain — filed the proper reports. I played it smart, Em."

"You always were the better cop, Ben." Emily nodded, staring out the glass occupying the upper half of the door. "Until now."

He joined her at the small window. The group gathered around his desk scattered. Two individuals paused outside the interrogation wing. One wore a white suit coat over khakis and had slicked-back hair. His companion, an aging African-American in a leather jacket, proceeded down the hall. Greasy fingers ran through his thin mustache.

"Is that Waters?"

Detective Horace Waters had served the precinct with distinction for over a decade. He'd transferred in from successful tours in four other major cities before settling on the Queen City as his home. Few held higher honors, including the role of hero to the masses.

"He took over the investigation, Ben," Emily stated. She backed him away from the door. "He's looking for you."

"Who was that with him?" The man in the khakis kept his head down. He turned for the exit without a glance back.

"Government spook. Didn't catch a name," she replied. She pinched the bridge of her nose while pacing the length of the room. Ben returned to the table. His concern grew with each step. "Listen, Ben. They secured a search warrant for the home. What they found in there —"

"They found a way inside?" Ben stood upright, excitement in his eyes. His stakeout had drummed up zero information. His resources, however, were limited compared to the department. If they'd managed to secure a warrant for the space — a chance to explore the structure from top to bottom? "I knew something was going on. What else — ?"

"Let me finish," Emily snapped. Thin eyes burrowed into him. "They found a body, Ben."

"A body? Who?"

"Our runner from that night," she answered. "That wasn't the end of it. DNA was found at the scene on the murder weapon. Your DNA."

"What?" he nearly shouted. The bottom fell out from under him. His world faded, the truth about the impromptu gathering at his desk suddenly snapping into focus. "I never —"

"I know. Ben, I know, but they —"

The door opened, which caused both to jump. Emily reeled, falling back from the entrance. Horace Waters grinned at the pair. He had a thick file tucked under his arm.

"There you are, Sergeant Wright."

"Yes, sir," she said. "I was just —"

Ben shook his head and she retreated farther along the wall. Both understood the implication, both recognized the situation he had created with his stakeout of the house on Wex. This was bigger than they'd imagined and Ben refused to risk her position on top of his own. He owed her too much, cared too much, to allow that to happen.

"Well, I'll take it from here," Waters said and glanced to the open door. Emily shuffled slowly into the frame, but she refused to vacate completely.

Ben pressed forward, the accusations running through his head. "Detective, I don't know what's going on, but I—"

"I think the evidence speaks for itself." Waters smiled. He circled the table and dropped the file in the center. A brush of his finger flipped the cover off and the images fell into view. Ben loomed over them, aggressively thumbing through each in turn.

There were dozens of photos of him from the last few weeks. They started innocuous enough. There were images of him outside the house, his nightly stakeout. With each new photo, a much different story unfolded. A large stash of drugs was uncovered in the domicile—meth, baggies of powder, and more of the solid crystal form. Scales and more paraphernalia were collected in the corner of the yellow-tinted entryway. Blood soiled some of the bags. When Waters flipped to the final image, Ben understood why. The man he'd chased inside the home on Wex that night weeks earlier was found dead in the living room. Blunt-force trauma to the back of the head made a clear case for the homicide detective. And the lab results of the DNA found at the scene pointed to only one other individual in the room.

"I didn't do it!" Ben snapped. He rushed to the far side of the table. The set-up took hold, the score obvious the moment Waters stepped foot in the room. "What the hell is this? What kind of game are you playing, Waters?"

"Ben!" Emily yelled. He stopped an inch from Waters' smug grin, then lowered his clenched fist. Her eyes softened as she fought back tears. "Don't."

Waters chuckled. He spun the overwhelmed officer around. A pair of cuffs snapped with finality against his wrists. "Listen to your girlfriend, pal. You're under arrest."

CHAPTER FOUR

The knob fought to turn. When it wasn't a physical obstacle before Metcalf, it was her own doubts. She stood in the doorway, the same way she had every day for the last two weeks, unable to penetrate the confines of her office—unable to move on from Grissom's death.

His belongings had been cleared out days earlier. She watched on, no words to temper the maelstrom swirling within her. No way of letting out the grief and the pain at letting him die. Without so much as a goodbye. Without so much as an explanation.

That was what it boiled down to in the end. She failed to understand—failed utterly and completely to figure out—the chain of events that led to the loss of this central figure in her life.

"Dammit, Jake," she uttered as she stepped into the silence of her office. Darkness held firm, the shadows deepening as the door shut behind her. In the distance she almost felt his presence, the same way she had each day since. Waiting to hear his voice, an inappropriate joke or a kind word whispered in her ear. Then the lights snapped to attention, wiping away the small hope left to her—forcing her to face reality.

"What were you looking for in there? What the hell were you thinking?"

No answers came in the weeks following their botched operation. The CDC swept the confines of Oliver Blake's lab, retrieving samples for study and removing the body of the fallen—the remains quarantined. Homeland Security oversaw the aftermath. All records were classified, and any chance at answers was buried in red tape. Each step was by the book—each for the safety of the country still reeling from the loss of twenty-three people in a callous act of terrorism.

Time passed in a blur. Even the funeral. Words were spoken by others. She had none to offer. Her words, her final order, had ended the man's life. What could be said to make up for that decision? What could she provide for the grieving, her own team included, to make up for that choice — one she would make again in an instant?

There was no secondary objective. No mission to retrieve a live sample. Their job had been clear: find the man and his records. Grissom had lied to the team and it had cost him his life. It was another question never to be answered.

"Why?"

Metcalf placed her briefcase next to the metal desk in the center and dropped her morning news atop the surface. Reports and status updates from the previous shift were shuffled aside, their number growing. She couldn't focus on them, unable to give them the attention they deserved. When she had lost Grissom, she not only lost the head of her field team, she lost her second-in-command: her deputy director. Now everything fell to her and she wasn't ready yet to handle things.

Not when the questions remained.

Metcalf left the desk and the backlog behind. At the rear of the office was a small credenza. A pitcher of water and four empty glasses sat upon a cloth in the center. She shifted the contents to one side and lifted the cloth to reveal a small keyhole. She slipped a silver key from her pocket into the waiting lock, the movement as natural as breathing.

A metal box sat within. Metcalf's chest clenched as she pushed open the lid. Hundreds of photos rested inside. The one on top was of a bright yellow farmhouse with a wraparound porch and hanging swing. Sitting on the swing, hand-in-hand, were her and Grissom. They smiled and laughed at the innocence of the day, the sheer peace of the moment.

It was a companionship that grew over time. Grissom had stood at her side from the very beginning, through the formation of the department, and the fights therein with every agency in Washington. She'd asked him for his loyalty and he'd answered with a decade of service and dedication to their cause.

Grissom did the asking after the photo that day at the farmhouse.

She never could say no to him.

"What the hell was *I* thinking, Jake?"

The box snapped shut and the concealed door closed over top. She shuffled the pitcher back into place after pouring a small glass to drown the contents of her stomach trying to fight their way to the surface.

Her work continued to wait. She loomed over it and let out a long breath, grateful when the door opened.

"Director?" the strong voice called before stepping inside. Stephanie Atwater wore a black sheath dress with a red blazer that covered her shoulders. A pair of flats dulled the sound of her arrival.

"Yes, Stephanie?"

She always brought a warm smile to the dismal space. A consummate professional, she never overstepped her bounds, keeping the chatter focused on the business at hand. It was exactly what Metcalf desired from her personal assistant.

"The Council is on the line."

"Of course they are." She'd avoided the matter for the last two weeks. Grissom had handled them in the past, the more tactful of the pair. Now it was another task passed to her with his loss. They called daily, demanding answers, pressing for information that either didn't exist or couldn't be explained. Everything available was already in the reports offered by her team and every member of the operations staff that had been present the day of the Blake operation.

An inquiry was set, a requirement in these situations. Part of her couldn't wait to finish the investigation to put it behind them. Yet, that meant leaving Grissom behind as well in a way. It was a conversation she wasn't ready to have.

"Take a message."

Stephanie nodded, hand to the door. "Is there anything I can do? Agent Grissom..."

She paused when Metcalf's gaze lowered. The mere mention of the man's name affected them all. The petite blond offered another nod, then slipped into the shadows of the doorframe.

"I'll let them know."

Left alone, Metcalf pulled the chair out and set to work. Morning papers from across the country waited for her. She dug through the news, stopping at the fourth periodical on the pile—the morning edition of *The Buffalo News*. The image screamed at her, fingers tightening and rending the photo into a blur of color under their grip.

Work would wait—questions, too, for that matter. Hell, the entire world could take a number. She failed Grissom but refused to do so again. This time she had the chance to make it right.

Her briefcase was back in hand and the door opened without hesitation. Her steps quickened, ignoring the swath of people milling about outside the Research room. She was nearly to the hall when Stephanie called, "Director?"

Metcalf stopped. "I'm taking some time."

Stephanie nibbled the corner of her bottom lip. She kept her voice low and away from the curious gaze of those around. "Far be it from me to question it, especially in light of everything, but is that wise?"

Metcalf smiled. Stephanie's concern was always appreciated—and always accurate. "Not in the least."

Sullen eyes accepted the response, a glance back to the phone and the recently ended call a reminder of the stakes.

"What is it, Stephanie?"

"They've assigned an investigator to look into the operation," she said.

"Who?"

"An independent consultant..."

"Hollis," Metcalf hissed. David Hollis had his hand in every government agency without the need of a badge. He had no place in this, yet somehow sifted through the rubble of their tragedy, hoping for opportunity. "Damn."

"There's more," Stephanie continued. "They've also hired a replacement for Deputy Director Grissom."

Deputy Director. Her assistant chose her words carefully. The new recruit was not intended to fulfill Grissom's other role as Head of Field Operations. They would not be a useful component to the department, but another bureaucrat to run numbers.

"Did they say who?"

"They didn't."

Metcalf nodded, and backed away slowly. She needed to be away from her office. "Send me the information when you have it."

"Where are you going?"

She lifted the paper, the image of the courthouse and the accused Ben Riley dead center on the page. "To settle some accounts."

CHAPTER FIVE

The bowl swirled beneath Wilson Dupree as he vacated every ounce of food and liquid he'd swallowed over the last two days. He heaved, and the final contents in his strained and agonized stomach splashed his reddened cheeks. He pawed at the remnants glued to his lips and wondered when it would end.

Eventually, the delicate balance in his gut returned and he settled along the bathroom floor of the convenience store. It was the closest stop within reach, the urge sudden and violent.

Staggering to the bathroom mirror, Wilson wiped the flakes of half-digested food from his face. He spit vigorously into the sink, hoping to remove the taste of the previous night's canned chili from memory. The very thought of it made him inch slightly back to the toilet bowl.

His unkempt hair covered his eyes and he pulled it back. His forehead burned at the touch. His eyes were swollen, bloodshot from a lack of sleep. The pain kept him up, and the inability to rest increased that agony in a never-ending cycle.

Wilson shook the dreariness from his eyes. Once-sharp green orbs faded to gray in the dismal lighting of the bathroom. He swiped at the dusty mirror, moving closer for a better look.

What is happening to me?

He pounded out of the bathroom and almost bowled over Juniper Flynn, the owner of Mainly Convenience. The mid-fifties attendant carried a tire around her midsection. Her left foot dragged behind the right in an effort to follow her one and only customer.

"Feeling all right?" she asked, her mouth only able to open on the right side, which caused her words to be muffled in Wilson's plugged ears.

"Don't worry, June," he said without looking. He continued to shuffle farther into the store. "I made sure to hit the target. Mostly."

He rounded the corner quickly and made a beeline for the medicine aisle. He bent low, his bleary eyes unable to make out the signage along the rows of products.

"Wilson?"

"Aspirin," he muttered, continuing through the different selections offered in the small shop. "Just need aspirin."

He paused near the front of the store. A large gap in products where the aspirin once sat stared back at him.

"No."

Hands pawed at the neighboring items. He shoved them aside, from eye drops to antacids, all in the hopes of finding a lost box of ibuprofen, or some Tylenol forgotten in a rush. Boxes crashed to the floor in his desperation and he collapsed along with them, then rested uncomfortably with his back against the display.

When he opened his eyes, June was holding out a bottle. "Here."

He snatched the pills from her, and snapped open the lid. Three pills shuffled into his shaking hand. He downed them without a second glance. His head pounded, and his fever pulsed, but he already felt better from the pills—the mental effect enough to keep him moving for a little longer.

"You too, then?" he asked as he fought for his feet.

June made no effort to help, her stocky frame barely able to carry her own weight, let alone the six-foot-two former star of the high school football team. She tapped her temple lightly. "Like a brass band against my skull. It's why I hoarded the good stuff."

"Thanks." He wiped his forehead free from a fresh layer of sweat. "Sorry about the mess. Don't know what—"

"Got nothing better to do today anyway. You should try and take it easy though, Wilson," June said. She moved for the counter. "Like the rest of town."

Wilson nodded at the emptiness surrounding them. Usually at this hour, people were swarming the streets. Instead, there was no one—no sound. Just the barrenness of the city. Wilson checked his watch, blinking hard to focus on the digital display.

"Taking it easy would be nice, June," Wilson said. "Too bad I'm late to pick up the kids. Again."

Primrose Elementary marked the western border of Bellbrook and the sister town of Centerville. The line in the sand also served as the barrier Wilson's ex-wife refused to cross, leaving him the duty of picking up his kids from school.

Lectured time and again for his inability to read a damn clock, the exhausted soul could hear the words from Assistant Principal Browne even as he pulled into the lot. He parked to the rear, hoping to avoid the glut at dismissal.

A dismissal that should have been ten minutes earlier.

Wilson checked his watch again, syncing up the timepiece with the Buick's clock. Both matched, yet no children raced down the street or around the playground to the left of the school. No parents waited at their vehicles for the rushing feet of kids excited for afternoon cartoons and junk food.

He shuffled from the car and the sun blinded his bleary eyes. The aspirin cut down the pain, but a humming remained behind his ears, piercing like the wail of an infant. He passed his neighbor's mini-van; the engine was running and driver's side door open with no one inside.

"Weird," he commented before starting for the front door to Primrose.

The office matched the scene outside. No sign of life. Paperwork littered the ground and phones were left off their base. The hall followed suit. Each step brought more anxiety to Wilson's sore chest.

"Josh?" He rounded the corner for the third-grade class of his son. Backpacks lay in piles near desks. Jackets remained in the closet in the back of the room.

"Where the hell?" He left the scene behind, and turned for the first-grade corridor. "Amy?"

He stood in the frame of the empty classroom, tears mixing with sweat. *Where could they be? What happened to them?*

Grabbing Amy's fallen Wonder Woman backpack and her purple raincoat, Wilson ran down the hall. A pair of glass doors marked the rear of the building. Beyond them sat picnic tables filled with desserts and treats for the kids.

"Fall Days," he breathed. He wiped the tears from his eyes. "I forgot about Fall Days."

It was a celebration every October. The school marked the occasion with a field day, one last real outing before the weather turned unpredictable. Josh had invited him to the party. How could he have forgotten?

A rush of wind greeted him when he opened the door. No other sound was heard save for the brisk air swirling and the random bird call caught in the draft. Wilson's eyes widened at the sight of the looming oak trees casting a long shadow over the back of the school. They spread from the exit, filling the periphery and extending far into the distance—a great forest.

"How did—?"

Wilson doubled over in pain, his hands plastered over his ears as a shrill cry filled his senses. His heart pounded to match his head, the threat of his skull splitting a genuine possibility for the man.

His knees slammed into the metal running at the base of the doorframe. Amy's belongings fell from his hands. He couldn't see, couldn't think. The act of breathing became a foreign task to him. He struggled with everything.

The sound grew to a crescendo until his struggle inevitably ended.

Wilson Dupree's hands dropped from his ears, and his arms fell slack along his sides as he stood. His eyes, once as green as the lush trees before him, faded to gray and then to white. Stumbling from the school, Wilson left the last remnants of his daughter's belongings and walked mindlessly into the forest.

He never looked back.

CHAPTER SIX

Ben ran his fingers over the bloodstain adorning his tie. He'd inherited it after his father's passing. The soft fabric comforted him, the large single blotch of deep red overlaying the black linen.

From the job…

He'd never wanted the job, never had the desire for the work his father always held in such high esteem. All he saw in it was darkness, one that swallowed up the man and his entire world too often. Despite his feelings, Ben followed his father's footsteps and served. He wore the badge proudly, trying to help where he could, to make a difference and bring some light back into his city.

He'd failed.

At the end of the trial, the testimony provided against him by Detective Horace Waters and a dozen others put the final nail in the coffin of everything that remained of Benjamin Harrison Riley. His life ended, and a new one was waiting outside in the form of two burly federal agents, there to escort him to his prison transport and a twenty-year sentence for crimes he'd never perpetrated.

Unable to handle the strain—the judge's harsh words booming in his ears—Ben took to the nearest restroom. He needed to be away from the storm of reporters, the lights from cameras, and the screaming of questions dizzying to him. Away from the mistakes made and the ignored advice that had led to his arrest. It was his one last act of defiance before all choice, all personal freedom faded and he became a number in the system, wearing nothing more than a prison jumpsuit.

It sounded slightly dramatic, but it helped him justify sitting in the narrow bathroom stall for the past thirty minutes playing with his tie. A knock on the door reminded him, however, that his time had long since run out.

"Occupied," Ben said. Staring deeper into the red splotch of blood on his tie, he almost caught his father staring back. The man had always judged—always hoped for more from the young man.

"I'm aware," a woman's voice answered, causing Ben to smile. "Your ass has to be numb by now."

He reached for the lock and clicked it over. The door swung open. "Like you wouldn't believe."

Emily rolled her eyes. Her arms crossed her chest as she leaned against the wall opposite the stall. Since the trial began, Ben cared to be around few people. Even fewer wished to be anywhere near him, considering the allegations against him. If anyone topped the list, though, it was the fiery brunette in front of him.

Ben struggled to stand. His black flats scrunched his toes, the pair two sizes too small. They were all he had. He fixed his tie along his white Stafford shirt, his handcuffs clattering with each movement. "You know you don't fit the gender-specific nature of this room, right?"

"Be glad it's me in here and not the escort outside you managed to piss off with this pouting business."

"I prefer to call it a deep contemplation of the universe. Sounds cooler."

"No it doesn't."

"It rolls off the tongue easier than 'coming to grips with my life being stolen from me and my face being plastered on every screen as the poster child for police corruption.'"

"Ben." Emily reached for his shoulder. He let her squeeze, feeling the warmth of her fingers, the joy of her presence for a brief moment before pulling away.

"You didn't have to stay."

"No one else is coming, Ben. I kept hoping, kept praying something would change, but... No one is coming to your rescue."

"I know," he announced over the rushing water from the faucet. He splashed the cool liquid along his cheeks. "I wish to God

I knew why."

"So do I," she said with a long breath. "I've been asking around—"

"Don't," Ben said. "Are you insane?"

"Hey," she replied in an attempt to calm his heaving chest. "You didn't do this. If you would have let me take the stand to tell the jury, to speak on your behalf, I would have."

"And you'd be wearing a new pair of bracelets as well, Em." He sighed, unable to find the words. His attorney had struggled to defend against the insurmountable evidence that appeared to crop up overnight. Analysts and experts in a dozen fields attested to the documents gathered by Waters. There were bank statements for accounts, both domestic and overseas. Witnesses Ben had never met, never knew, yet somehow were able to relate intricate details of the crimes laid at the former officer's feet. Everything and everyone pointed at Ben's complicity and his guilt. All because of his damn curiosity.

"Why couldn't you have stayed away, Ben? Why couldn't you have listened just this once?" Her voice was bitter. He knew it wasn't directed at him, but at the chains along his wrists. She took his hand in hers and squeezed. "It doesn't have to be this way. I can fight this. We can—"

"No."

"This is your life, Ben."

"And they took it from me, Em. They took it and there wasn't a damn thing I could do to stop them," Ben said, his voice cracked and strained. She swiped at the tear in his eye and he fought to smile. A lesson learned from his mother, long since gone from this world. To find the light in the moment, even in the darkest of times. He admired her in that regard, dreamed of better days at her side. "Hey. I'll be all right."

"How?"

"I still have you, don't I?"

She nodded, fighting back her own tears.

"I'll figure this out, Em," he said. They inched toward the door and the sound of impatient steps approached. "We'll figure this out."

"Together," she finished.

Ben's hand hovered over the handle to the men's room, unable to pull the door open. His thoughts dimmed. His enduring smile struggled to return. When he'd joined the department, when he'd caved to the wishes of his father to pin the badge to his chest to make a difference, he had done so with the conceit that he would make the world a better place. That through the abuses of power, through the ignorance of violence, Ben Riley would stand as a force for change. *For the job* instead of from the job, as his father always said.

Only, the job had won out, taking it all away from him.

They entered the hall, the escort quick to confirm the cuffs were still intact around his wrists. Emily trailed at his side as they started for the transport parked out back. Reporters were pushed aside until the quiet of the building returned. Emily stopped at the end of the hall. The guards rounded the corner to check out the situation. She fixed the hair from her face, tucking the thick strands back effortlessly. "Ben..."

She pulled him close. Her lips fell on his and he held her for a long moment, one he never wanted to end. Comfort and safety from a single sensation. When the kiss ended, it stayed with him. From the gleam in her eyes, Emily matched his reaction.

"You'll visit?"

"Ben, I—"

"And don't steal my stuff."

She fought for a smile. "Your junk, you mean."

"Those comic books will be worth millions one day. Guaranteed."

"I'll let you know after I sell them," she replied. "Kidding."

"Be safe, Em."

"You too."

His escort steered him through the building. He glanced back, trying to wave, trying to hold onto the moment and her image for a second longer. But she fell away into the shadows, like so much of his world since his arrest.

Ben took a sharp breath. His hands grazed the bloodstain along his tie. He stepped ahead of the two burly agents. "Any chance for a bite to eat before we head out?"

"Quiet now, Mr. Riley."

"No speaking? You really don't know me at all."

The bus waited beyond the exit. The door was open, the gloom of the evening settling over the lot. One of the guards left his side to exit the courthouse. He reached into his pocket and removed a slip of paper, handing it to the waiting driver. When he returned, he offered his partner a slight nod.

"This way," he muttered. The guard shoved Ben toward the emergency stairwell, the sound of metal grinding as the exit opened. The prison transport's engine revved before starting down the block.

"What? Where is he going?" Ben stopped in the doorframe, shaking loose from the guard. "Guys? Pretty sure we just missed the bus."

The pair stood stock-still, one holding his hand close to the earpiece tucked on his right side.

"How about an answer?" Ben called once more. "A grunt? Anything?"

"Yes," one answered. Ben started to speak, but was waved down by the other agent as the first continued his conversation. "Sending him up now."

"What the hell is going on?" Ben demanded without success. They barred his exit from the stairwell, forcing him up the first flight without a word. "Who the hell were you talking to back there?"

Silence was the only response. Their climb extended up floor after floor until reaching the rooftop. The agent in the lead propped open the door then shifted aside. A key fell loose from his pocket, and he unlocked the cuffs.

"She's waiting for you."

Ben waded into the evening air, heavy with impending showers, and found her near the ledge. Auburn hair and sharp blue eyes, the confident woman stood straight and bold in a long skirt and flats.

She grinned at his arrival. "Let's discuss your future, shall we, Mr. Riley?"

CHAPTER SEVEN

"Coffee?" Slender fingers extended one of a matched pair to the confused newcomer. Ben followed her exacting gaze, almost hidden by her hair whipping around in the early-evening wind.

Ben shook his head. "I'm partial to smoothies, actually."

No annoyance sat in her face. No emotion lost at all in her stance. She simply turned to place the second cup along the ledge, then took a moment to savor some from her own beverage.

Most of the roof offered little in the way of movement. A slight platform extended from the top of the stairs along the northern side of the courthouse. Small drops of rain and the cold wind of autumn kept Ben closer to the stairs than he cared to admit.

"Look," he called as the woman returned from the ledge. "I'm not sure what the game is here—"

"No game," she said with a disarming smile. "Just a job offer."

Ben let out a short laugh. She failed to join him. Sharp blue eyes followed his awkward movements. She wore a tan raincoat over her skirt. Her umbrella sat perched beside the door. Always prepared for the occasion--even when it came to standing alone on a rooftop with a recently convicted criminal.

His escort was gone. The twin behemoths that had shoved him up here in the first place no longer blocked his escape. The thought occurred to make a break for the door—to flee into the city and hope the law never caught up to him. His life would still be over, however. There were also the woman's eyes which held him in place—all-seeing and all-knowing. She read his every reaction before he even had a clue what was running through his own thoughts.

"I don't know you," he announced.

"But I know you," she said. "Benjamin Harrison Riley. Five-year veteran of the Buffalo Police Department. Not your first choice. Your father wanted it though. You stepped up when he fell ill." Her eyes wavered and her head bowed in thought. "Cancer. He went quick."

Ben blinked hard. He hadn't heard his father's condition told so succinctly. More importantly, he'd never realized the impact his father's passing still held on him. Douglas Riley had been a tough man to love, one who'd expected better from all those around him. From the woman he married, to the son he raised alone after her passing, Douglas' ambitions were set upon all he encountered.

The startled man with the bloodstained tie left the comfort of the stairwell for the cool air whipping over the courthouse. He stared out over the city. His father's beat. Not a single route, and not a simple neighborhood, but the whole of Buffalo.

"For as much as you maligned the work, you made it your own," the woman continued, joining him at the edge of the roof. "A solid record. Two commendations. A fast track to promotion."

"Gone now," Ben said. He kicked at the pebbles beneath his shoes. "Not that I'd ever really wanted it."

"What *do* you want?"

Ben stopped, hesitant for a brief moment. Then he laughed. "Wait. Is this my fairy godmother moment? Are we talking about my shot at a kick-ass pair of glass Skechers and a rave with my Prince Charming?"

"No," the woman said. The first glimpse of irritation rested behind the declaration. "This is your chance to keep making a difference. To not give up on your life when you've done nothing wrong."

"I already fought that fight. I lost, and everyone in this city seemed to want it that way," Ben said, pointing out at the sky-line.

"This doesn't have to be the end." The woman paused. She put the coffee down, placing her hands at her back. "It shouldn't be. Not for stumbling across something bigger than you knew."

"Wait," Ben muttered. "The house. You know about the house?"

"What you saw, a level of technology beyond anything we're currently capable of? They want to keep it that way."

"Who?" Ben pushed for more. This was his life on the line, his entire existence, and she knew the truth behind everything he had witnessed that night. "If you know anything, any information at all, tell me. Your testimony—"

"Would be as easily written off as your own," she replied, eyes a sea of blue against the gray of the open sky.

"They killed a man!"

"For what he found inside." She nodded. "They could have easily done the same to you. Killing a cop, however, is a messier job. Too many questions. Better to bury you: lock you in a cell and let time finish you off."

"You can take them to the house. You can show them what is—"

"They've moved their operation. The keypad you described in your statement is gone. They planted their narrative, falsified evidence—photos, documents, reports—all to maintain the illusion of control. You're not the first, Ben. You won't be the last, unfortunately."

"Who is doing this to me?"

"I don't have all the answers, Ben," she said. "Horace Waters was involved in some way, but he's disappeared as well. Every link in the chain has been either fortified or removed. What I'm offering you is the chance to help me find answers we're both looking for."

"I have to go." Ben moved for the door. "You have to tell them, to make them see that this was a mistake. That sending me to jail isn't right."

"Right has little to do with anything," the woman answered. "Sending you to jail silences you. I'm sure it won't be the end of what they are willing to do to you to keep you that way. Keep pushing and your silence will be more permanent, I assure you. Take my offer and you can have your chance against them, a chance to make a new life. You can set your own path."

What *did* he want? What life was there for him? He'd always lived through others or for them—from his father to the precinct and even the people of the city. What was there for him in any of it?

"This job of yours," he said. "What does it involve?"

"Field work for my department."

"Field work?"

"As an agent."

"An agent?" Ben squeezed the bridge of his nose. "This… this whole thing is insane. I don't even know your name."

"Susan Metcalf."

"This is insane, Susan Metcalf."

She nodded and extended her hand. "Sanity is a matter of perspective."

The world sat in front of him. There were two options before him. A chance to keep breathing fresh air and find the answers for why he'd lost his life, or to feel the cold metal of cuffs against his wrists once more as he fell into darkness.

"Ben Riley lives or dies by *your* choice. Not theirs. What will it be?"

He took the offer in hand and shook. "Your department. Does it have a cool name?"

"Not in the least," she said with a laugh. "Have you ever heard of the DSA?"

CHAPTER EIGHT

The sound of their phones stirred them. One vibrated against the grain of the dresser across the room and the other rang from the kitchen. They fought the pull, listening to the rhythmic hum in stereo. Finally, Ruth surrendered to the day. She crept away from his embrace for the cold floor.

Lincoln struggled to open his eyes, grateful for the view and the thin stream of sunlight slipping through the curtains. Bare skin danced across his field of vision. She reached for the phone and the item slipped between calloused fingers. The notification, short and to the point, caused the joy on her face to fade.

"That the call?" He shifted for the edge of the bed, where he grabbed for his fallen shorts.

Ruth nodded, letting the phone clatter against the dresser. "Metcalf's back."

For weeks they'd waited for word from their errant boss. Weeks were spent dealing with the aftermath of their loss. Their grief endured, thanks to the ceaseless inquiries from sister agencies wanting nothing more than a scapegoat for the whole affair. It broke them, reliving the nightmare of watching Grissom die before their eyes, unable to save the man who had done so much to rescue them from their previous failures.

Loss brought them closer together. More than Lincoln and Ruth ever could have imagined. Shared grief had turned to consoling, turned to something unexpected and wonderful. Now, all had been shot to hell by a single text message.

"There's a briefing at 1800 hours," Ruth continued.

A sly grin escaped and he pulled her close. A kiss ran along her neck. "Then there's no rush."

She returned the kiss then pushed him away playfully. For a second, there was hope in her eyes: hope that this, their connection of the last few weeks, would continue without question. It vanished, like so much else in the light of the morning sun.

He understood immediately, catching her hesitation which turned to remorse at the act. Metcalf was back. A briefing was on the docket followed by routine and obligation. Life as they once knew it returned, obscuring the one they'd built while the DSA had been on pause. They had finally caught their breath, only to see it drawn away at the department's leisure.

"Linc," Ruth started. She grabbed at fallen clothes and rushed to cover her beauty from view. "I have to head in."

Work meant a return to reality. Back to normal—for the good of the team. For the DSA. Always pushing the cause ahead of their own lives. Lincoln understood, and had believed in the job for years since his recruitment. Their short time together, however, had opened up a new path. One closed now, by all appearances.

"I get it."

Her shirt fell in place and she pulled it taut. A hand ran along his shoulder, massaging scarred skin lightly. "She's put me in charge of the field team. With Grissom gone…"

The memory stuck with them. Grissom's shadow sat in every room, in every interaction. He was the reason they had connected and the reason it had to end at the same time.

Lincoln shook his head. He held her close. "You're nervous. Don't be. He picked you for this."

"I can almost believe it when you say it."

"Believe it."

She kissed him, hard and fast. He fought for more, one more second, but she fell away and started for the door, the shadows swallowing the light in the bedroom.

"I'll see you there?"

"I'm right behind you," Lincoln said.

The door closed, leaving silence in the apartment. Lincoln grabbed some clothes from the dresser and tossed them in the bathroom. He needed a quick shower, not that he cared to move with any sense of speed or purpose. He merely stood in the center of the bedroom, the strewn pillows and rumpled sheets the only remnants of their time together.

A sigh uttered, Lincoln reached for his shoulder holster, hanging off a nearby chair. His Glock waited inside. He pulled the cold weapon loose and ejected the clip—full and ready for the day ahead.

"Back to it, then," he muttered. He slammed the clip in place. Then he headed for the shower to wash away the serenity of his downtime.

There was more work to do.

CHAPTER NINE

She read the same line again. Each word, taken in turn, failed to penetrate. Morgan sipped at her coffee, more than willing to keep to the same page of the book. It wasn't that the book was inherently bad or overly convoluted. It was the act of reading itself. Sitting still for long periods of time had never suited her, though she continued to make the attempt. Sitting drove her anxiety level through the roof. Downtime was for people who didn't have better things to do.

Not for Morgan Dunleavy.

The coffee helped. So did the fresh air. The corner cafe in downtown Bethesda overlooking the Round House Theatre distracted her enough to force her to relax for a moment. To take another day, another moment for herself.

She hated it.

When the text came through from Metcalf and the meeting was scheduled for a return to the status quo, part of Morgan wanted to jump from her seat in exclamation. It was time to go back to work, not that she hadn't been there every day to check in on things. Stephanie and Zac offered little in the way of updates. The hub gave her less to accomplish before shuffling her back into the autumn wind and a book she barely recalled even after staring at the page for minutes on end.

She needed work, the energy and the constant movement it provided. She needed anything to keep her from thinking; from dwelling on the past—and on Grissom.

Dammit, Jake. Why did you have to die?

The same question she'd asked every day since the man's fall. He had saved her from a life of emptiness, fed her a new purpose and propped her up. He'd deserved to be saved, deserved the same second chance he'd offered her. She had failed him.

They all had.

Satisfied with the message, Morgan closed the book. She lifted the marker meant to hold her spot from the table and shook her head, constantly forgetting about the damn thing until it was too late. She sifted through the pages until surrendering and placed the thin divider in the front of the novel. There would be time later for reading.

After grabbing her coffee, Morgan stopped at the shadow passing overhead. It blocked the blazing sun, the rare treat of the October sky before the snows started.

"This seat taken?"

Rounding the table, a man reached for an open chair at her right. He stood just shy of six feet tall with a head of perfectly placed black locks, which he shifted away from wide eyes. His smile greeted her. His coffee and pastry was already in place on the table.

"Go for it," Morgan replied with a glance. She snatched up her belongings and stood. Her height eclipsed the young man, which surprised him for a moment. "I was just—"

"Oh." Disappointment spread. "I was hoping you'd stay."

Hazy brown eyes beamed at her, eyebrows cocked at the invitation.

"Can't," she shrugged. His hand caught her arm as she passed, halting her departure. She waited. Her sharp look caused his fingers to recede. Leaning against the chair, the young man whipped his hair to the side.

"You're here most days," he said, hand to his hip. "I've seen you. Noticed you. Thought you'd noticed me the way you were staring, so I came to say hello."

"Didn't notice. Can't stay."

The confidence melted. His invitation dismissed casually.

"Duty calls," she continued, pushing for the exit.

"Bad timing, I guess," the man muttered. "How about—?"

She didn't peer back as she rounded the open fence along the sidewalk. She didn't want the company, didn't care for it. All it did was remind her of the past, opened the door to reflection on her mistakes. She refused to repeat them, refused to entertain the thought of a connection. All she required was work.

"Another time, then," the young man called as he shrank into the background.

She slipped between staggered traffic. Her sedan waited at the corner. Neatly trimmed nails grazed the handle and paused. She peered back to the table and the young man's invitation. He sat, any sadness immediately forgotten at the approach of another woman. She joined him, accepting his smile and welcoming the conversation ahead.

"Another time," she whispered in the autumn breeze. "Another life."

The days of pick-up lines and cheap dates were over for Morgan. They belonged to other people. Work was all she had left.

Exactly how she preferred it.

CHAPTER TEN

It was all waiting for her when she returned. Metcalf stood in the doorway to her office, hoping for a change. Hoping against every likelihood that the last month had been a fiction, and that reality had reset for her. That Grissom was still alive somehow.

Seeing the paperwork piled atop her desk and the webs of neglect in the corners of the room made the situation clear. She had tried to flee from her problems, tried to abandon the fact for a fiction that would never come to be.

Now she was back.

The field team was notified. That had been her first priority. Then she went about putting everything back in its place. Department heads compiled updates for her review, though Stephanie had kept her abreast of many of the trials of the past few weeks. Hollis' interviews of the staff took the top spot, much as the news pained Metcalf to hear. The man was a spider crawling along the skin of every government agency — waiting for an opportunity to seize any discord.

It was to be expected.

Everything fell to routine. Metcalf took up her chair behind her desk and settled to the paperwork left in organized chaos upon the metal tabletop. Routine requirements such as supply requests or paid time off had once filled her with a sense of accomplishment — a need for control. Everything filtered through her hands, every aspect of the department. From the mundane need for more toilet paper in the women's room to maintenance contracts on the MRI machine in the subbasement lab. All were hers to know and oversee.

Minutes into her long-awaited return a figure marred the

frame of her door. The slight rap against the metal failed to attract her attention, lost to intel reports from the research team on a longstanding investigation which had been closed during her absence. Before she realized it, he was in her office, heavy-soled shoes pounding against the tile.

"You're back," he announced, this stranger in her midst. He wore a thick green sweater-vest and tan khakis. A snow-white beard bristled along his cheeks and chin to match his tightly trimmed hair. Deep, recessed eyes echoed the man's age—somewhere in his mid-to-late fifties. Greg Sullivan had no place at the DSA, no qualification to enter the premises, yet somehow had managed to sneak through Metcalf's carefully crafted defenses. Much had lately and it needed to stop.

"When Stephanie said you were in here I almost didn't believe her," he continued, inching closer to the desk. He carried a stack of fresh reports for the pile. Placing them on the metal chair opposite her own, he stood upright and extended a hand. "Greg Sullivan. Your new Deputy Director."

"So I've heard," Metcalf said. She stood and accepted the hand with a firm shake. Stephanie had brought the assignment to her attention soon after her departure. Her dedicated secretary filled in many of the blanks that came with Sullivan's appointment.

He was a career politician, though career was the wrong word in his case. During Sullivan's first term as a congressman he had run afoul of a scandal, one starting with a small financial exchange and ending with his resignation in a fairly public setting. Since that time he'd somehow managed to work his way back into the graces of the political system. He had consulted for various firms over the years until being tapped as Deputy Director of the DSA.

"I want to thank you for handling things in my absence," Metcalf said, offering the chair. He removed the paperwork, letting it rest at his side as he joined her under the dim glow of the desk lamp. "I'm sure these weren't the best of circumstances to start under, but I'm hoping we can move forward in a positive manner."

"Nothing would give me greater pleasure, Susan," Sullivan said. "I have plenty of experience in this arena and can prove an invaluable resource as I'm sure you'll discover."

"Of course," she replied.

"Did you find what you were looking for?" he asked, right leg crossing over his left at the knee.

"I'm sorry?"

"Your absence. Did you—?"

She shook her head. "Just some personal business. Nothing pertinent to the department."

"I see," he said. He held out each word, waiting for more.

Her hands folded before her. She was patient in her silence. She'd found enough answers in her time away, and more questions thanks to her visit to Buffalo. Sullivan, however, wasn't Grissom, and any trust between them would have to be earned. "Bring me up to speed, Greg."

"Operations have been placed on hold for the moment."

"I've lifted that hold," Metcalf answered.

"Oh," Sullivan said in surprise. "With the recent inquiry and the Council's wishes I would have thought—"

"Council's wishes?"

His hand ran the length of his beard. He seemed to enjoy the back and forth. She noticed it in the wry smirk he struggled to hide—the control held thanks to her absence. Knowledge she was not privy to despite her frequent contact with Stephanie during her time away.

"They believe, and it has always been their belief, that the DSA serves better as a research-based operation. Field work—"

"Is a necessity to find the answers to certain situations," Metcalf finished. A decade of the same argument, one she'd fought tooth and nail against with each meeting held. One Sullivan was more than willing to surrender in his opening salvo. "Our field team handles the more dangerous operations, those that our sister agencies can't."

"I understand. However—"

"Greg," she intoned, fingers clasped tight. "There are hundreds of cases filtered through this building on a monthly basis. While most require merely a second glance to offer local departments more insight, there are dozens where we can take an active approach. We need *more* boots on the ground, not less, and I would appreciate it if you conveyed that message to the Council."

"I see."

"You're new, Greg, I get that."

"Not so new. I assumed their approach to our meeting was dubious, at best." He palmed through the paperwork at his side and retrieved one thick leaflet. The file landed atop her piles with a thud.

"What's this?"

"The Council pushed a meeting with me rather than you to further their agenda. That's not my job here. I'm here to help you."

She paged through the contents. Sullivan had compiled a thorough report with field requisitions and operations statistics from the last few years. Every page highlighted the higher success rate achieved at the DSA compared to other agencies with many more resources.

"Mr. Modine assisted in putting it together. It made your request for more assets in the field quite clear."

"I… appreciate that," she muttered, taken aback. "How was it received?"

"I believe our friends at the FBI and CIA agree with your assessment. Stallworth at the NSA is on the fence. You can forget about Homeland and the rest."

"Bureaucratic nonsense."

"That you despise. I'm starting to get a sense of that, at any rate," Sullivan said. He slipped comfortably deep into his seat. "Now, Stallworth was telling me over lunch last week that—"

"You had lunch with him?"

Sullivan paused, the question surprising him. "Yes. I do eat."

"A work-related lunch away from the rest of the Council?"

"Now, Susan—"

"No," she snapped. "You're new and I respect your experience, but that's never the way we've done things in the past. No side meetings. No dealings. Ever."

Her absence had been a mistake. She could tell from his grin and the way his hands sat tucked in his pockets. Sullivan came from money, from power and influence. It was a world very much unlike her own. He played the game his way and he needed to learn what worked for her and what didn't.

Her glare stuck with him until he acquiesced. "Of course."

"Thank you," she said. "Anything else?"

He retrieved the unread report and pondered the question.

"Ah, yes. They had more questions about your recent whereabouts following—"

"It was personal."

"Right," he drawled. "They were simply curious as to—"

"It was nothing," she reiterated. "I had the time and I took it. End of story."

"Okay."

She waited. "And?"

"There were more questions about Agent Grissom."

She had her own—more than she cared to admit. Unfortunately, no more answers were coming. "Final reports are on the server for the Council's review. Those include testimonies provided to that nightmare, Hollis, during my absence."

"Susan…"

Before he continued a knock rattled the door. Three short raps, and then the metal slab slipped from the frame and a demure young woman in slacks and a flowery top stepped inside.

"Sorry to interrupt," Stephanie said. Her blond hair was tucked in a bun at the peak and a clipboard covered her chest.

The obstacle did little to dissuade the enormity of Sullivan's excitement at her arrival. "Not a problem, my dear."

"What is it, Stephanie?" Metcalf asked.

"Mr. Riley is here."

"Good. Give us a minute."

Stephanie nodded. She kept her focus on Metcalf to avoid Sullivan's grazing stare. Satisfied with the answer, she exited the office and closed the door.

"Riley?" Sullivan said.

"Grissom's replacement." She reached into her briefcase and passed the file across the desk into his waiting hand. "Benjamin Riley."

"Riley?" the newcomer repeated.

"Former beat cop. Familiar with him?"

"Not at all," he grumbled, eyes to the file. "Looks to be a good fit for the team?"

"Looks to be."

Sullivan snapped the report shut. "Wonderful. I'll be sure to inform the Council of your decision. You know how they like to be kept abreast of any changes."

"I do." He headed for the door, but Metcalf stopped him.

"Make them aware that we need more agents, Greg. That's your job here: to promote our operation. We can do more. Make them see that."

Sullivan nodded, a slight bow in his acceptance. The lie came in his silence. His footsteps carried into the hallway, leaving her to her work. Metcalf sat at her desk and sighed. Ten years she'd put into building the DSA. With each breath she felt it pulled from her. Sullivan was but a prelude.

Quickly and efficiently, she tossed aside the backlog from her absence. She turned on her sleeping terminal and clicked on the directories locked at a command level. Files, once shared between her and Grissom, were no longer safe in the hands of the stranger now occupying her old friend's office. Sullivan's name was noted multiple times since his arrival, his fingerprints all over her files. He'd asked for trust, and she had none to give — not now, and possibly not ever. She made a list of the directories and slipped them into her pocket, wondering what the man's game was and how much time she had to figure it out before it became too late.

CHAPTER ELEVEN

Ben tapped impatiently along the worn tile with his feet. His toes scrunched tight in the black loafers, his one and only pair now. His wardrobe had been lost to limbo in the blitz to depart Buffalo.

At least he still had his father's tie.

He cradled the precious object, running his fingers along the bloodstain in the center. Nothing felt right, nothing felt safe—despite Metcalf's assurances. Two days locked away in a hotel room under heavy guard did little to dissuade that sensation, though the *Back to the Future* marathon and hour-long steaming hot showers made the situation as amenable as possible.

He dropped the tie as the door to Metcalf's office opened. A gentleman with a thin, white beard and dated green sweater vest glanced his way before edging for the receptionist's desk.

Stephanie, a woman with bright beaming eyes and an altruistic smile, noted the presence with a less-than-gracious look. The two bantered quietly. Ben did his best to ignore the uncomfortable stance of the pleasant aide who had offered more conversation to him than any other since his departure from his hometown in a shroud of mystery. Government goons made for terrible company, something Ben didn't realize until offered a seat and a smile by the young blond.

He kept his eyes locked on the ajar office door. Inside, Metcalf clacked away at the keyboard. There was a power in her presence, something hidden in the way she sat behind her desk. More waited beneath the surface to be discovered, much like the DSA itself.

Heels clicked beside his wayward stare and he realized

Stephanie was next to him. "She's ready for you now."

"That makes one of us," Ben replied. He jumped to his feet, his toes regretting the act, then trudged his way inside the office. The door closed soundly behind him, though it did little to stir Metcalf, who continued to work.

After a long moment she paused, removed her reading glasses, and ushered him to the chair across from the metal desk cutting the room in half. "I'm glad you made it."

"Not much choice," he said as he settled into the chair. "Or maybe my armed escort just forgot to list my options. Makes a guy wonder if he made the right call."

"Just being cautious."

"And?"

Metcalf raised a glass of water to toast his arrival. "To new beginnings and all that, I suppose. Would you like some?"

"No, I'm good."

She took a sip before returning the glass to the tabletop. "Now, you are aware that you are to have no contact with your former associates, friends, family, mail carrier, and so on, correct?"

"I figured as much." Though he'd held a slight hope for a different edict. Emily Wright thought he was in prison. Everyone he'd known in his former life believed the same, but when it came down to it only Emily mattered. She didn't deserve to worry about him, not when he was still free—not with the smallest glimmer of a chance for them to be together again.

Metcalf read his disappointment. "It's not only to protect you, Ben, but them as well. Until we know who set you up, the risks are too great."

"I get it."

"Good," she said, pushing away from the desk. She started for the door. "Walk with me."

The pair exited the office and made a hard left. Behind him stood the lobby and entrance, complete with security checkpoint. Three guards paced the area, two of whom he recognized as part of the escort from the courthouse. Moving on, Metcalf passed a cubicle farm spread across a spacious room. Syncopated typing filled the air, and the sound of fingers keying with extreme precision echoed all around them. Dozens of analysts stared at monitors. Each viewed reports, exploring news items and clippings while taking notes of relevant information before moving to the next.

"I still don't know what this is," Ben said to fill the silence offered by Metcalf.

"That only means we're doing our jobs well."

"Okay," Ben said, holding out the word. "How about a simple one to start. Where am I?"

The trip had been maintained under the cover of secrecy, to make sure his background check or whatever thoroughness Metcalf hinted at was reached to some degree of satisfaction. Again, his friendly neighborhood government goons—not that he called them that to their faces—appeared less inclined when it came to details. Or pleasantries. Or any type of welcoming attitude in any regard. Not even a fruit smoothie for his trouble.

"Bethesda," Metcalf smiled. "Maryland."

"I know where Bethesda is," Ben lied, not meeting her eyes.

"Right. This facility was formerly used for storage—old files and artifacts."

"Like—"

"No. Not like *Indiana Jones*."

"Not a fan?"

She sighed, heading deeper among the cubicles. "Before that, this place was a weapons bunker. We've retrofitted it to our needs."

"Homey."

She stopped. "Not asking you to live here, though there are living quarters on the fourth level."

What else is in this place? Ben wondered as they continued. "Speaking of housing…"

"Stephanie has all the details."

"Your secretary seems out of place here."

"How so?"

"Too nice, for one. She just here for show?"

Metcalf laughed. "No. Though secretary doesn't quite sum up her role here. Trust me, Mr. Riley, there is more to Stephanie Atwater than meets the eye. The same can be said for much of our operation."

"So don't call her a secretary. Got it."

"Smart man."

He shrugged. "When it suits me."

"Your escort also helped put together some belongings from your apartment. They gathered some clothes and mementos. Things that would go unnoticed should anyone search your place after your tragic downfall."

"Sounds like the title of a Lifetime movie based on me," Ben muttered. "*My Tragic Downfall. The Ben Riley Story.*"

"What else?"

"It's your tour, Metcalf."

"Director."

"Director," Ben corrected his error. "Lead on."

She did, taking them to the far side of the open space. Large displays lined the wall. They offered a glimpse at each task being worked on at that very moment. Departments ran along the left, as well as personnel assigned to each case. Priorities were marked in bright red, others denoted in black. New work filtered through consistently.

"Officially, the DSA is a catch-all. We handle the overflow while working under the auspices of a governmental Inter-Agency Council. We follow the edicts and regulations of our sister agencies, funneling resources and manpower where necessary."

The so-called sister agencies marked the end of each row on the monitors—from the FBI to Homeland Security and more. Specific field offices described the locale as well as points of contact. Each were monitored and regulated by department heads inside and out of the DSA facility from the looks of the monitors.

"Why not keep it internal?"

Metcalf led him under the rear wall, where a wide stairwell took them to the lower level of the facility. "In today's day and age of public scrutiny? Feeding it to us helps everyone else keep their bottom line clean when they are called up to Capitol Hill for a spanking. The DSA doesn't suffer the same litmus test of efficiency as everyone else."

"Why?" The question caught in his throat, and he read her smirk well. "Because no one knows about the DSA."

She clapped her hands lightly and he offered a bow. "Very few. Yes."

To the right of the stairs they passed a series of laboratories. Small windows along the doors allowed Ben to peer inside. Keypad codes were required for entry. Multiple people worked diligently within, wearing masks and other protective gear. Some tested chemicals, and others ran medical scans, all with the latest technology in the field. No matter what else Metcalf said about the DSA, it was well-funded.

Beyond the lab, they stopped in front of a fully functional gym filled with exercise equipment. A woman in cargo pants and black boots benched twin barbells larger than Ben's head. She lifted the bar off her chest in constant repetitions. There was no struggle, only an intense focus to accomplish the task. Unwilling to distract her, Ben quickly moved away from the room for their next stop.

A gun range extended around the first bend in the corridor. Five stations, tucked behind soundproof walls, led to targets hundreds of yards away. Only one station was occupied. The man inside fired off an entire clip in a matter of seconds. He dropped the weapon, securing a second in the blink of an eye before repeating the barrage on the waiting target.

Ben shook his head. Metcalf's steps led him around another corner. The lower level was an enormous loop with the research team positioned above their heads. More labs and storage rooms were staggered along the long corridor, but he paused before pressing on.

"Wait," he said. "You said 'officially.' What about unofficially?"

Metcalf nodded. She leaned along the left-hand wall. "The DSA is called many names; its current iteration as the Department of Special Assignments is nothing more than a designation offered by the Inter-Agency Council. The original one, the one used by those that formed the organization as field agents like yourself, was the Department of Scientific Anomalies."

"Seriously?"

Metcalf grinned. "Technology advances daily. We're on the cusp of breakthroughs on so many fronts. Medical. Engineering. Artificial intelligence. We have the capability to mine the depths of the oceans or journey to the stars above. Unfortunately, not everyone is looking out for humanity's best interests."

He didn't need to be told. The same was true with everything he'd witnessed at the house on Wex. This was more of the same, but on a much grander scale.

Lost thoughts brought something else with them. "Spokane."

"I'm sorry?"

"It was in the news about a month or so back," Ben continued, trying to piece it together as he spoke. "A viral outbreak of some kind at a coffee shop? They never said what it was or who was behind it."

"We handled it," Metcalf replied. Her gaze shifted down the hall. Along the right-hand wall were a series of plaques. Six rows adorned the wall, names and dates etched along each bronze square—a memoriam for the fallen. "Not without losses, I'm afraid."

Ben surveyed the plaques. The most recent made up the top row. The closest one to his position displayed the name JACOB GRISSOM with a date that lined up with the Spokane incident. Ben trailed the names back through time until settling on the lowest rung.

"I see dates from the seventies here."

Metcalf joined him. "The DSA became official a decade back, but there were some, like yourself, that had the notion to serve above and beyond."

"Is that what I'm doing?"

"Don't you see it that way?"

Ben didn't have the answer she wanted, or even one of his own to share. When his father had fallen ill he'd made a promise to continue the man's work, but to do it his way. Instead of seeing the darkness, Ben viewed the world with optimism that was perpetually beaten down by the events of his career, but never shattered—sometimes lost, but never completely forgotten.

Across from the memoriam was a single door, locked and protected by a retinal scan and keypad entry. The word ARCHIVE adorned the wall next to the security measures. Metcalf input her code and the door clicked open. She held it for him so he could look inside.

Processing ran along the left side of the room—a loading dock for new equipment or departing evidence to their various offices. Twin terminals and a server room stretched along the right-hand wall. Ben wondered what secrets the millions of terabytes stored on the DSA's mainframes held, what answers could be found in their database. Every mystery that had been solved and hidden away from the public—from the Kennedy assassination to Roswell and so much more.

Beyond the open area at the forefront of the section sat the archives themselves. Files were stored on shelving units that stretched into the darkness. The shelving took up two rows down the center of the area. The outskirts held evidence lockers and the so-called artifacts alluded to by the proud director, who monitored his reaction from the door.

"How?" Ben asked. "You're talking about science and technology, intricate subjects I have no experience with—like, at all. I was a cop and not exactly the best to begin with."

"Ben," Metcalf started. "I have more cases flooding through these halls every second of every day. I have hundreds of analysts looking at the world from a different perspective than top federal agents who have hundreds upon hundreds of hours of expertise in their areas. These analysts come from all backgrounds, the technical to the mundane, all in the hopes of solving the peculiar and the unthinkable.

"Those are the cases my field team takes head on, which you would be part of. I don't need lab coats and technical advisors. I need grounded investigators, able to read a situation and act accordingly. I need smart, capable people willing to do the right thing no matter the cost."

"Metcalf…"

Before she could correct him, a voice shouted from the end of the hall, "Director!"

She reached for Ben's shoulder. "We'll have to put a pin in that for now."

"Director." A frumpy man with dark stubble along his chin fought for breath as he skidded to a halt. "There you are."

"Here I am," Metcalf answered. "Zachary Modine. This is Agent Riley."

"A new field agent?" Zac asked with a scoff. "No one told me."

"I'm telling you now," Metcalf said, teeth clenched in an awkward smile. "How about a hello for the man?"

The new recruit held out his hand. "Ben."

Zac replied to the greeting with a grunt, but ignored the hand. The overweight tech wiped his brow and pushed closer to his superior. "I need you to look this over, Director."

Metcalf rolled her eyes. "You'll get used to Zac. Some do, anyway. What is—?"

"Something happened in Ohio."

The confused director paused. "Save it for tonight's briefing?"

"Briefing has to be now."

"Why?" Ben asked.

"Pretty sure I already said it, new guy. Something happened in Ohio."

CHAPTER TWELVE

The briefing room occupied the end of the hall on the lower level. A large cherry table sat in the center, chairs positioned on all sides. Displays covered the walls. Diagnostics on current operations and briefing notes were fully loaded with the help of the staffers working tirelessly at desks on either side of the door.

Zac rushed away from the approaching pair to finish last-minute preparations. He brusquely shoved past Ben without a second glance. Ben shrugged it off, playing Zac's behavior to the man's low blood sugar, but he couldn't help wondering if more was involved.

What was he doing here? Law enforcement had never appealed to him, and his time as a beat cop had served only as a constant reminder instead of a revelation to some higher calling. Through his job he witnessed the worst of humanity. Petty theft, domestic disputes, murder, and the like. Humanity scared him, left him cold and empty, yet here he contemplated defending it once more.

He wondered if the other agents felt the same. Three sat at the table, waiting impatiently. There was the strawberry blond, hair cut short, from the weight room earlier. Her boots rested on the table as she pored over the shifting displays relaying information. Behind her sat a muscle-bound black man, fingers delicately yet rapidly snapping a Glock back in working order with his eyes closed. Across from him a tall woman with ebony skin and curly black locks down over her shoulders sipped her coffee. Her deep brown eyes caught his stare before dropping back to the table.

Metcalf waited for his focus. "Hang back here."

"I'm sorry?" Two more staffers rushed through. They passed off graphics to the typists. Zac leaned over them and compiled notes.

"There will be plenty of time for intros later. Right now though? Stand, sit, squat, whatever. Just shut up while the briefing is in motion. Sound good?"

Ben rubbed at his neck. "Quite the team builder."

"I'd like to think so," Metcalf said. "Still haven't answered my question though."

"You mean the one directed to a six-year-old stuck in a parent-teacher conference?"

"That's the one," she said with a smirk. She tapped her heel to the ticking of her watch. "Becoming more appropriate by the second."

Ben nodded, hands in the air. "Yeah, no. I'm good."

"You sure?"

"Go be bossy," Ben said. He pointed at the waiting crowd. "Somewhere over there."

Metcalf straightened her jacket and stepped inside. The agents at the table paused to stand. Metcalf noted the protocol and took her position at the table. Ben settled in the back corner as the last staffer joined the meeting and closed the door behind her.

The lights dimmed. Ben squinted and the center of the table lit up. A holographic three-dimensional image hovered over the cherry conference table: a blue and gold emblem carrying the DSA moniker atop an eagle. Twin swords stood guard on either side.

Metcalf pulled her chair in. "Bring us up to speed, Zac."

"Right."

The display shifted once more to an aerial view of a small town. Demographics and general information ran along the right side of the screen.

"I thought the briefing wasn't until six?" the woman in the cargo pants said. She cast her thumb toward the back of the room. "And who's the suit by the door fiddling with his tie?"

Ben chuckled and let go of his tie. He didn't realize he had been playing with it, or that anyone had noticed his arrival. "I'm—"

Metcalf shook her head. "Don't worry about it, Agent Heller.

Zac?"

"Bellbrook, Ohio," Zac started. He clicked through images no doubt taken from the town's official website: happy families and bright tourist spots to visit. Nothing of relevance to the current situation that Ben could tell. "Population just north of seven thousand. Home of the Sugar Maple Festival."

"Seriously?" the tall ebony-skinned woman asked.

Zac shrugged, and his face reddened. "Ohio, remember?"

"Sounds downright evil," the man holding the Glock said. He chambered a round, the sound echoing in the closed room.

"Let the man finish before you start picking targets, Lincoln."

Lincoln removed the clip and smiled. "Better talk faster, then."

Agent Heller threw the man a glare, then dropped her boots to the ground. She slid her chair in hard against the table, hands neatly folded and all business in her posture. "What's the deal with Bellbrook?"

"It's not there anymore," Zac answered.

"What?"

The hefty tech let out a short laugh. "Sorry. It's there. Of course, it's there. What I meant was this."

The display shifted. Satellite images turned to real time photos of the town. There was nothing but empty streets and storefronts, as well as vacant homes. Cars remained present, but they weren't driving on the roads. Some were parked, others no longer even that, almost like they'd drifted to a halt— abandoned in mid-drive.

"Twenty-four hours ago the town went dark. No phone traffic. Television signals. All we have are these images from one of our friendly neighborhood satellites at the Department of Defense to show us more nothing. No people to speak of. None that we've seen, anyway, and we've been receiving updates for the last three hours. The city is a dead zone."

"So where are the people?" Metcalf asked, hand to her temple and glasses tight against the bridge of her nose.

"That's what I'm saying." Zac took a breath. "They appear to be, well, not there anymore."

"Mass exodus?" the lanky agent with the coffee intoned.

Lincoln grinned. "Boredom became too much?"

Zac rolled his eyes. He flipped the display once more. Three images showed on the screen. Two were young women and the last was of an elderly gentleman.

"Some missing person's cases were filed at first. The first was over a week ago. Small numbers. Routine stuff. But they increased to a point where they started to look pretty darn suspicious. Then, like a light switch, they just stopped."

"They were located or—"

"No," Zac stopped Agent Heller's question. "There just weren't any more submitted. We tracked all signals in the area and they all seem to have gone dead." Bar graphs and charts filled the screen. Agent Heller opened her personal tablet to view them directly. "Using our NSA resources we reconstructed all cell tower info from the last week."

Each day's results showed prominently on the screen. They appeared normal with chatter on all fronts noted and recorded. "People are, of course, glued to their phones, so the information is easy to attain. Even in Ohio. Apps, photos, social media, calls too, if you can believe that. All tracked and recorded for our viewing pleasure."

"Until?" Metcalf rolled her finger to push the tech along.

Zac nodded, focused on the previous day's results. The graph was empty; the chart displayed no information at all.

"Nothing?"

Metcalf removed her glasses. "Local authorities have been notified?"

"They were, yes."

"And?" Irritation crept into Metcalf's voice.

"No response."

"Why is this coming our way? If anything, this should be Homeland's problem, right?" Lincoln's question drew the attention of everyone in the room. He threw his hands up in defense. "What? I'm not trying to pass the buck or anything."

Agent Heller grinned. "Someone wants more downtime."

"I happen to *like* my downtime," Lincoln said, smirking at the strawberry blond for a long moment.

Their colleague lowered her coffee. "Yeah right. Making bullets and eating take-out from the same diner every night. What a life."

"Don't knock it till you've tried it, Morgan," Lincoln said.

"All right, people," Metcalf interjected. She stood, but leaned heavily on the table. "Answer Lincoln's question, Zac."

"Right," Zac said. He stared at the ground. "I don't know."

"What?" Metcalf said in disbelief. "This must have come through channels."

"It didn't, actually," Zac replied. "This just popped up in our priority system. No idea how, but it seems to have been directed solely to us."

"No one else is aware? Homeland? None of the Council?" Zac shook his head. Metcalf rapped her fingernails along the cherry tabletop. "You're looking into it?"

"Of course, yes," he said. "I could toss this to official channels if you'd—"

"No," she said quickly. "It's ours. It came to us, so we'll handle it."

"But if you're worried about proced—"

"We'll handle it, Zac."

Agent Heller dropped the tablet to the table. "What's blocking the signals?" The tension between Metcalf and Zac fell away as eyes returned to the charts displayed overhead. The agent stood, pointing at the moment of activation, little more than twenty-four hours ago. "No radio waves, no television signals. Nothing, right? You said Bellbrook was a dead zone, but that isn't accurate. There's something covering them up."

Zac stared mindlessly, joining the rest of the room in silence. Then he grumbled and buried his hands in his pockets. "Yes. Right. Exactly. I obviously can't pinpoint it from out here, but I believe—meaning the research team and myself—theorize another signal is overlapping or cutting off all others. Something we don't know how to track through our current systems."

"For what purpose?" Metcalf inquired.

"No idea."

"So you don't really know *anything*," Ben announced from the back of the room.

Zac's jaw hit the ground. Metcalf's ire was audible in the form of a deep growl slipping from her lips. All around the room the attention diverted from the briefing at hand to the sound of a newcomer to the affair.

"What... the... hell?" Zac said, struggling for anger in his confusion.

Ben stepped forward. "Hey there."

Metcalf squeezed the bridge of her nose. "Not what I would call the best ice breaker. Everyone? I'd like to introduce you to our newest agent, Benjamin Riley."

Ben grinned. "I did try to keep quiet."

"Well, I appreciate the attempt." Metcalf circled the table. She showcased the players all sizing him up with their silent gazes. "Say hello to the rest of the field team and your direct supervisors. Morgan Dunleavy, Lincoln MacKenzie, and Lead Agent Ruth Heller."

"He's filling Grissom's spot?" Ruth asked, irritation on her face. It forced Lincoln to laugh and Morgan's eyes to fall to the tabletop. "You should have told us, Metcalf."

Zac offered a slight nod, one matched by the surrounding analysts. This wasn't how Ben had hoped to step into his new role—one he knew little to nothing about or how to make it work.

"I am now," Metcalf said. Her gruff attitude added to the tension in the room. "This isn't a democracy, Agent Heller. I handle personnel and recruitment when it comes to—"

The ebony-skinned woman with the deep brown eyes stood from the table, and silenced her superior in the act. She approached the new recruit with the bloodstained tie, towering over him in stature.

"Morgan," she said softly. She took his hand and gave it a firm shake. "Welcome to the team."

"Ben," he said. "Already established, I know."

"Ruth," grumbled the woman in the leather jacket. She continued to study the display, merely raising a hand in acceptance of his presence.

"That a Ruger LC9?" Lincoln asked. The black man was shorter than Ben, but hardened, his muscles packing muscle of their own. Not that he needed it with the twin pistols strapped to his shoulders. He held out a hand. "May I?"

Ben withdrew his sidearm from the holster and laid it upon the man's waiting palm. "Be my guest."

Lincoln caressed the instrument more like it was a Stradivarius instead of a weapon to be used only as a last resort. "Well maintained. Not cheap either." He flipped the pistol around, catching the barrel, and returned it to Ben. "Full clip?"

"I try to keep it that way," Ben responded, curiously.

Lincoln shook his head. "Good luck with that around here."

Metcalf cleared her throat, eyes scanning the crowd. "All right, everyone. We are in the middle of something here. Anything else, Zac?"

"Nothing," the tech said. "Not until that signal is taken out. Then we can assist from our end."

Metcalf nodded. "You heard him. Pack your bags. Flight leaves in an hour. Let's see where the fine people of Bellbrook are hiding."

CHAPTER THIRTEEN

Silence was the watchword of the day, something Ben quickly noticed from his new colleagues. No one spoke about Bellbrook or the situation within. Ruth ran through notes. When questioned about what they headed toward, she snapped a fast response, unwilling to engage. Nerves rattled her and no one pressed. This was new terrain for her as well. For them all, it seemed.

Lincoln listened to music—Ben assumed it was something classical like the organ music at a hockey game. His machismo struck Ben as false, or maybe it was his belief that club-wielding alpha-males couldn't possibly still exist in the modern age that was false. Lincoln must have read his mind, flipping him off for his effort. Morgan stared out the window, a book on her lap. She picked at the pages every once in awhile.

Who were these people? Out of everyone qualified to handle situations as unknown as the one currently affecting the people of Bellbrook, how had an organization like the DSA settled on these three? What made them special? Ben couldn't see it and doubted his colleagues could either. They merely answered the call, hoping to do their best.

The landing at Lunken snapped them back to the situation at hand. Before long, the team found their rental car waiting and hopped inside. Arguments flew over the driver's seat, Lincoln's attempt for control immediately overruled by the ladies of the squad. Ben stayed quiet, falling against the leather of the SUV's back seat.

He remained undecided about the DSA, and about working in law enforcement in general, if this even qualified as that. The

DSA was just like every bureaucracy. They dressed the department up as covert ops, but there was required paperwork, as well as superiors pressing an agenda. Did they make a difference in spite of that? Were they able to effect change in a positive light? What did they fight for? Better still, what was *he* fighting for as a member of their field team?

Route 675 opened up and the Suburban streamed along the double-lane highway west toward Bellbrook. Traffic surrounding Cincinnati flowed heavy, but with each exit passed—with each suburb and township left behind in their travels—fewer and fewer vehicles surrounded them until at last they were alone.

"You keep looking at your tie."

Ben shook his head. The green by the side of the road reminded him of day trips with his family as a child, but Ruth's voice had ended his nostalgia. His fingers rested on the bloodstain marring his otherwise black tie and he dropped it along his chest once more.

"I like this tie."

"It certainly has character," she remarked, eyes in the rearview mirror.

"Thank you," he said. "It also serves to remind me how insane my life has become."

"You get used to it," Morgan said as she stared out her window. Lincoln let out a low chuckle from the front seat, a Steelers cap resting over his eyes.

"Seriously?" Ben asked, incredulous. He inched to the edge of the seat. "No real intel from local authorities and we jet right over? Four agents with no backup or a way to call for backup once in this so-called dead zone, which we can all agree needs a name change unless Anthony Michael Hall shows up."

"Or Stephen King," Lincoln muttered.

"I actually would not be surprised by that."

"In Ohio?" Morgan shook her head. "Never happen."

Ben shrugged. "Neither should a disappearing town, but say hello to the new world."

"What do you really want to ask, Riley?" Ruth's question hung in the air, a soft, knowing stare in the mirror.

"What makes you think I haven't asked already?"

"We all went through the confused, sarcastic phase of recruitment. The doubts… well, let's just leave it at that, I guess."

"Well, while we're on the subject—"

"Don't even try asking her," Lincoln interrupted as he pointed to Morgan, who returned to the window, head resting along the cool glass.

"Why not?" Ben pressed. "I'm willing to share."

"Not necessary," Lincoln said.

"Why?" Ben stopped. Ruth slammed harder on the accelerator. She raced against an invisible clock to reach their destination, or perhaps to avoid the conversation entirely. Morgan did the same, unwilling to pull away from the scenery. Only Lincoln engaged. His cheerful grin irritated Ben. "Ah. You already know."

"Looked you up after the briefing," Lincoln replied. "I can't believe you sat through that farce of a trial. If it was me, I would have killed every one of those bastards for what they did."

What they did… Just like that he was back in the courtroom, surrounded by friends and colleagues calling for his blood. Betrayed and broken, his entire life stripped from him. A career he had never cared for, decisions never his own, yet he appreciated the opportunities—especially now that they were gone.

"You have no idea—" Ben paused. He settled against the seat, hand to his tie.

Lincoln laughed. "All I'm saying, new guy, is—"

"Knock it off," Ruth snapped.

Lincoln tried to respond, locked in her glare. Instead, however, he swallowed the words and retrieved his lost hat.

"Okay," Ben said, pushing through his own failures. "So I get to be an open book and everyone else is in the restricted section?"

Ruth sighed. "Fine. Former NSA. I didn't play by the rules and ended up here."

"I'm guessing there's more to that story."

"Definitely is," Ruth groaned. Her knuckles turned white against the steering wheel. The engine shifted gears as the SUV rumbled along the highway. "You'll live with the disappointment."

"Fair enough. Agent MacKenzie?"

Lincoln's gun slipped from the holster and he set it on his lap. He grazed the cold metal. "Secret Service," he answered, his voice lost to memory. "Six years. My charge didn't make it."

"Assassinated?"

"No, Riley," he seethed. "A damn head cold."

"Morgan?"

She shook her head, shadow falling over her from outside. The random shrubbery decorating the side of the road faded and they entered a lush forest. A tall canopy of oak trees surrounded them on both sides, full of leaves fighting against the approaching winter.

"That's it, then?" Ben asked. "Really?"

Ruth turned, irritation building to anger. "Yes, Riley. Team-building exercise over."

"Great. Four rejects versus Bellbrook. Can't wait."

Lincoln cracked a smile. "That's why we're the DSA. The Department of Stupid Asses."

Ben laughed. "Please tell me our badges say that. Wait... we do have badges, right?"

Lincoln nudged Ruth, who groaned. She reached into the side compartment of a nearby bag and tossed Ben a plastic package, the contents spilling out on the seat between him and Morgan. Ben collected the items, flipping open the badge to see the same emblem from their briefing. The DSA logo shone against the paper. Ben's name was marked in bold black font next to the image — like it was meant to be there.

"Zac's working on a new version of the logo," Lincoln said.

"Why?"

"Something about not being iconic enough," he grumbled. "Kid's got too much time on his hands."

"That should turn out well," Ben remarked.

"Exactly."

They laughed as the forest ended. A large sign decorated the side of the road and Ruth sighed loud enough to draw their attention.

"Get serious, people," she said. The sign beamed in the afternoon sunlight, a picturesque village along the bottom and the words WELCOME TO BELLBROOK at the top. All fell silent as they entered the city, wondering what was coming for them.

Ben reached for his tie. "We're here."

CHAPTER FOURTEEN

The Suburban slowed, following the winding trail through Bellbrook. Ruth took her time. She scanned the streets ahead, the same as the rest of them. Open fields in front of Primrose Elementary turned to the town proper. Businesses occupied blocks upon blocks, some decrepit and all abandoned.

Cars dotted the road. Some were parked. Others halted along mailboxes or against buildings and other vehicles. It was as if the occupants simply stepped out and never looked back.

Red lights held no meaning other than to act as a momentary pause, allowing them to search for some sign of life. No one walked the sidewalks. No one raced with glee around the playground at the end of the road. There was no one in the restaurants or the shops in the quaint village setting.

"It's empty."

Ben turned away from the window. He caught the sadness in his companion's eyes reflected along the glass. "Morgan?"

"I mean, I knew it from the briefing, of course. It just seems so—"

"Empty."

She nodded, fixated on the scenery of downtown Bellbrook.

"Where do we start?" Lincoln tapped at the gun in his lap, anxious. "Circle the town for signs of life, split the town in quarters, take them on foot? How do you want to play this, Ruth?"

"Local authorities are standard procedure for us, but I don't think we're going to get anything there." She pointed to the precinct across the street. The front door flapped in the wind. Clouds rolled in behind them—dark, like their spirits.

"Looks like no one's home," Ben whispered, reaffirming their feelings.

"We need to start somewhere," Ruth said.

Lincoln smiled. "Well, I know I could go for—"

"Don't," Ruth snapped.

"I'm just saying—"

Her eyes thinned and Morgan jumped between them. She leaned close and patted the man's shoulder. "You know how he is when he doesn't get his daily microwavable burrito. No matter how inappropriate the situation."

"It's tradition," Lincoln retorted. "Like a good-luck charm or something."

"Or something is right," Ruth mocked. The rental left the road, skirting the curb at the corner of Main and Franklin. It came to rest beside the gas pumps that took over most of the parking lot in front of Mainly Convenience.

Lincoln clapped his hands. "You're the best."

"We're not here to satisfy your *Fifty Shades of Mexican* craving, Linc," Ruth said. "Look."

The roadside sign buzzed, pointing to the store. The doors were closed, but the open placard remained along the glass. No people presented themselves in the form of employee or customer, though the shop held one thing none had seen anywhere else upon arriving.

"The lights are on," Ben said.

"Exactly," Ruth replied, then reached for the door handle. The cool wind rushed in as she headed out.

Lincoln followed suit. "Just means the juice is still running for a late lunch."

Morgan rolled her eyes and the pair in the back of the Suburban joined the rest of the crew outside. The wind whipped at Ben's coat, so he buttoned it up, locking his tie within. Sidearms were drawn and Lincoln led the pack toward the door.

"Slow it down," Ruth called. She pushed to the front of the caravan. "I'll take point. Lincoln?"

He nodded and resumed their momentum to the store. Her hand fell on his chest and she shook her head. She pointed to the rental resting quietly by the gas pumps.

"No," Lincoln exhaled, finally following her lead. "No way in hell."

"I need—"

"You need me in there," Lincoln said. "Watching your back."

"Mister burrito…"

"Was joking," he said. He pulled her away from the others. Anger never entered in his voice. Instead, there was disappointment. "I ain't joking about this."

"You will be watching my back," Ruth said. "On lookout."

"Don't—"

She turned away. "Keep watch, MacKenzie. That's an order."

Lincoln swallowed his response. His tongue ran the length of his stark white teeth. "Got it."

Ruth rejoined the others, letting out a long breath as she did. She made for the door, but paused on the left side. "Agent Riley?"

Ben shook his head, hesitant at the sound of the title. "Going to take some getting used to with that."

"Just get through today," Ruth said. "Manageable goals."

Ben took the right with a nod. They paused at the door to ready their weapons for what might lie within. Morgan took up position in the center, gun in hand and medical kit strapped to her shoulder, the first aid symbol a deep red over the black case.

A doctor? Ben thought. He should have learned more ahead of time about those making up the team, about anything more pertaining to those he now entrusted his life to in the desolate town of Bellbrook.

His ignorance had to end. So did the distraction.

They opened the door and Morgan led the rush inside. Ben and Ruth followed close, each covering the angles. Ruth nodded to Ben and he accepted the unspoken directive, taking the far side of the store while she cut across the first aisle near the windows.

Morgan hung back, offering an overview of the store and a means to relay any information necessary to Lincoln, who paced the parking lot while he scanned the surrounding area. Ben, in the meantime, checked over the counter for signs of life before eliminating each aisle as he tracked toward the back of the shop.

He left the narrow hall for the moment, Morgan covering him the entire way. A sound broke through the silence. Ben's shoes squealed to a halt. Ruth glared at him from the row of freezers at the end of the shop. He shrugged, then crept toward a series of three doors along the wall across from the windows.

"Where?" he whispered.

Ruth pointed to the first door, next to the twin restrooms. The word OFFICE was written in red marker on a piece of lined paper and tacked to the hollow door. The humming sound grew louder with each step. Sweat beaded along Ben's palms.

Ruth joined him at the door, ready as he gripped the knob. He twisted hard to open it. The sound of a computer fan past its prime greeted them. It was not the source of the humming sound, though.

That came from a rotund woman collapsed on the floor.

Morgan was there before they could call for assistance. Her sidearm was tucked away and the med-kit was in her hand before she entered the cramped quarters of the office. Ben backed off, though Ruth continued to train her weapon on the woman, the first sign of life found in the vacant town.

"Ma'am?" Morgan asked, her voice rising over the pained moans. She crouched at her side and her hands eased the woman to her back for a better view. "Ma'am, can you tell me—?"

"Can't you hear it?" the woman yelled, eyes wide and faded to white. "Can't you hear that god-awful noise?"

"What noise?" Morgan pressed. She tried to pry the woman's hands from her ears. The nametag pinned to her chest read JUNE. "What noise are you hearing, June?"

The woman shook her head and pushed Morgan away.

"June? I want to help," she said. "We want to help. What can we—?"

The woman screamed, lashing out. She backhanded Morgan to the floor of the office. The lanky agent's head slammed soundly against the desk along the back wall.

The woman in her fifties was on her feet. She rushed for the door before they could react. Her scream forced them to hesitate. Ruth raised her gun but not fast enough. June slashed at her, leaping from the office like a rabid animal.

The lead agent cried out. She dropped her sidearm and clutched her sleeve.

Ben rushed toward her. "Ruth!"

The rotund woman shoulder-checked Ben, blasting him into a nearby shelving unit. Packages of chips spread along the aisle as he fell atop them. June reached the end of the store and turned for the front. She stopped at the sight of Lincoln circling the perimeter.

Before Ben could stagger to his feet she was already back-tracking for the rear hall and the secondary exit. Ben hesitated to pursue. Instead, he turned to the cursing agent on the ground.

"Ruth?" he asked as he tried to help her up. "Are you —?"

Morgan shuffled between them, rubbing her head. "Let me take a look."

"Morgan, I—"

"Go!" she shouted at him. "Get her!"

Ben nodded and was gone, racing off after June. The back door to the store slammed against the building and bounced back, forcing him to elbow it away before he cleared the frame. June was barely in sight. She had cut through a neighboring alley across the street.

His feet screamed with each step, but he refused to halt as he charged against the wind into the alley. Garbage bags piled from the week lay on both sides, and he skirted them, leaping over the ones pulled down by the raging breeze cutting through the thin path.

He was two blocks over when he returned to the street. June was in the distance, picking up speed instead of slowing down. The stocky clerk carried twice his weight and half his stride, yet she increased her distance with each block traveled.

"How the hell is she moving so fast?" It mirrored his own thoughts and he turned in surprise at Ruth having caught up with him. Her hand clamped against the wound along her arm, but it did little to deter her.

"I've got this," Ben said, the pair side-by-side. "Morgan should be looking at that cut."

"She's checking out the office. This was more important." They rounded another corner. "Now where's—"

"There."

June cut down another alley almost three blocks out and they followed. It curved around the back of an office complex and turned into a shallow parking lot. When they rounded the corner they were on the next street over.

They found only emptiness waiting for them.

"Wait," Ben huffed. "What?"

"She's gone? How?"

A baseball diamond stretched before them. Chain-link fences

rattled along the dugouts on the first and third baselines. The outfield extended to another fence in the distance, the forest marking the western border of Bellbrook beyond it. No one was in sight. There was no sign of June's departure, no clue as to where she could have gone, especially with no cover close enough to reach in the time it took to close the distance.

Ben wiped the sweat from his brow. His other hand rested along the trunk of a tall oak tree positioned behind the backstop at home plate, the lone shade in the entire park.

"Where the hell did she go?"

CHAPTER FIFTEEN

A closed malt shop welcomed them back to the main road. Boarded windows and spray-paint decorated the front. The milkshake-shaped sign leaned precariously over the street from a wind storm. Across the street two collections agencies vied for office space, blocked in the center by a private investigator that should have reconsidered using the word *dick* in bold letters on the window.

Bellbrook's story was unknown and remained so for Ben and the rest of the DSA field team. It was a history yet to be revealed, circumstances left to little more than circumspect guesses and theories rather than tales told over campfires at the abandoned drive-in theater at the end of the lane or in the modest kitchens vacant in all homes they'd passed.

What had happened here? Their one lead since arriving had vanished, the mysterious Olympic-level track star locked in the body of an overweight citizen named June. Her disappearance was yet another mystery in a town rapidly filling with them.

Ben blamed himself. Had he tried hard enough? Had he run as fast as possible? Doubts were understandable. They were all he carried with him ever since his arrest. He'd accepted Metcalf's offer to learn who framed him and why, but also to figure out what life he truly desired. Not defined by family or circumstance, but to make the choice on his own and see where the chips fell. Only, he was the one falling, leaping in the deepest, darkest well imaginable. He wondered if he would ever view the light again.

He wondered if the DSA had been the right choice or if it had simply been the only one.

Ruth wavered beside him. Her left hand was locked on her right arm, covering the scrape gifted by their missing lead. Her skin was pale and her feet shuffled along the loose pieces of concrete.

"You all right?" Ben asked. He tucked away his doubts. There were other concerns, including his new colleagues.

"Yeah," Ruth said breathlessly. Her knees wobbled beneath her. Before she could fall, Ben's arms outstretched to catch her. She shook her head, wiping tiny beads of sweat from her brow. The cut on her arm pulsed red, deep and dark. A bruise started to form around it.

"You want to try that again?"

She stood and pushed away from him. "I said I'm fine, Riley."

Lincoln stared from the parking lot of Mainly Convenience. Catching his growing glare, Ruth shuffled faster toward the rest of the team. Ben held back, his feet aching inside his much-too-small loafers.

"Right. Nice chat," he grumbled before following in silence.

He shouldn't have been surprised. They didn't know him any more than they knew the situation surrounding the small town in Ohio. No history tied them together, no story connected them. They were mysteries as well, closed books unwilling to share the past or embrace their future together.

Hell, did he even want them to? Did he want to open up to these people? What the hell was the DSA anyway?

Morgan stepped out of the store behind them. She tore off a set of plastic gloves and dropped them in her med-kit. A small blood sample joined them in the case before she closed it up. Halfway through, she paused, noticing Ruth's arrival. A bandage was in her hand before a greeting could pass, though Lincoln was beyond that point.

"Seriously?" he said to the new recruit. "She's gone?"

"Lincoln..." Morgan started.

Ruth pushed through him for the SUV. Lincoln reached for her. "Ruth, what's — ?"

She knocked his hand away and continued to the back of the rental, where she slammed her fist against the panel.

Lincoln looked on, hands to his hips. "What the hell?"

"Let it go," Morgan snapped. She rounded the vehicle with a

bandage prepped. Ruth waved her off, refusing treatment.

"Whatever," Lincoln muttered. His eyes, once sharp and cold, turned soft. The moment didn't last. "That's fine. I want to hear how rookie of the year over here got outrun by a woman twice his age and weight."

Ben shrugged. "One second she's in front of me and the next? Poof."

"Now what?"

"We look for June," Morgan replied.

No one spoke, letting Morgan's answer hang between them. Lincoln rolled his eyes, then scanned the neighborhood for other signs of life. Ben rubbed at his neck. Tired of the silence, Morgan let her medical bag slam against the ground.

"She might need our help."

"We offered it to her, remember?" Ruth said, her words bitter and pained. "Besides, we have a whole town playing hide-and-seek with us."

"Ruth's right," Lincoln continued. "We can't focus on one mental patient."

"Maybe she wasn't, Lincoln," Morgan said, arms crossing her chest.

"What do you mean?" Ruth held back Lincoln's retort with the wave of her hand.

"She complained of a sound only she could hear."

Lincoln held up a finger. "I said mental patient already, for the record."

Morgan shook her head, ignoring the man. "What if there *was* a sound?"

"The signal." As she said it, Ruth's eyes ran back into her head and she reached for the safety of the SUV to keep her upright. Her breath caught in her throat and Morgan rushed to her side.

"Ruth," Ben called, attempting to help.

Lincoln stopped him, hand to Ben's chest. "Back off, Riley."

Ben knocked him away. "Lincoln, I have had about enough of your —"

"Not surprised," Lincoln relayed. "You didn't seem like the type to stick it out."

"You sanctimonious…" Ben cocked his fist back.

Lincoln egged him on further with a deep laugh, forcing

Morgan to jump between them. "Guys! Enough!"

"No," Lincoln cackled. "Let him. I'm not about to let this newb get us killed. We have to go from Grissom to this guy? No training? No experience in the field and I'm supposed to trust him to watch my back?"

Ben rebuked, "And you're such a staunch soldier, is that it?"

"You have no idea who I am or what I've been through, you piece of—"

A hand fell on Lincoln's shoulder. Ruth trapped the angry agent's eyes and locked them in place. "He's doing the job, Linc. Same as us. Same as Grissom did."

Lincoln let it settle over him, not only her words but her presence. She fought to smile and he accepted it graciously. Pulling back, he leaned heavy against the side of the SUV.

"Okay," Lincoln said. "So tell me what we've got, because near as I can tell we have no damn clue about what happened here or where to even look. What the hell job we working here, Ruth?"

"The one Metcalf gave us, Lincoln," she said. "So shut the hell up."

This wasn't the norm for them. The questioning and the doubts were more than those Ben held for an unknown organization and a stranger situation. This was a new situation for the rest of them as well—a new chain of command. No one was used to the idea of Ruth giving orders. That included the strawberry-blond with the bad attitude.

Morgan intervened, their shared question on her lips. "So how do we stop this, Ruth?"

"We find the source."

"We can do that?" Ben asked.

Ruth mulled the question over for a moment before springing to the rear of the rental. She opened the trunk and rummaged through the requisitioned equipment. Bags shuffled on top of bags, others tossed into the back seat to make room. Ruth opened each in turn to take inventory. Her eyes danced around the contents of the vehicle, assessing and understanding their situation as best as they could.

She closed the trunk and sat along the bumper. "We'll need more tech than I packed. But we can do it, yes."

"I saw an electronics store a couple blocks back," Morgan

said.

For the first time that day the group appeared together, truly together for the next move. It was in Lincoln's stance, in Morgan's smile, and burning bright in Ruth's eyes. She held the keys before her.

"Let's move, people."

CHAPTER SIXTEEN

Gadgets and More stood in the middle of a deserted plaza. Shuttered stores occupied the ends. A grocery store took the vast majority of space offered by the complex. They circled the back, the entrance barred by a locked gate and combination padlock. When they reached the front, the foursome exited their vehicle.

The storefront window had been shattered, immediately raising their awareness. Sidearms were drawn and flashlights replaced the faded sun as clouds rolled in from the west. Ruth took the lead once more, Ben at her side. He did his best to ignore her unsteady steps and the way her hand reached to her temple more often than his own to his tie. He didn't need the argument, but more than that, his focus was lost on the status of the shop.

Glass littered the inside, not the walkway outside. "Someone might still be in there."

Ruth nodded, cautiously entering. Her leg arched over the window display, cheap toys and games used to draw in the family crowd. Morgan and Lincoln covered her entrance. Ben followed the trail of glass, catching sight of small flickers of blood along the remnants.

"We'll take the right, Riley."

"Got it." Ben caught a thin glare from Lincoln.

"Definitely not staying back this time," the gun-toting agent said.

"Wouldn't ask you to," Ruth said.

He shifted left. Morgan scanned the lot for more than the empty cars scattered throughout. Then she followed, glass cracking beneath her feet.

"Anything?" Ben asked, moments later. Ruth surveyed the

nearby displays; the newcomer assisted as well as he could with his flashlight.

"Not yet."

"Couldn't Zac get a fix on the signal?"

Ruth stopped. "Not outside the zone. Being in the epicenter of whatever signal is cutting off communication with the outside world allows us to piggyback and therefore figure out its location."

"Then why isn't he here with us?"

"Listen," Ruth whispered sharply. "This isn't your beat, and this isn't some game. Metcalf might have sold you on that unique perspective crap back in Bethesda, but what it really boils down to is the fact that we are here because we are the ones willing to take the risk. Without question. Without hesitation. That's the job."

"Good to know."

"We need to move for the back," Ruth said, looking past Ben for the others inching down the left-hand side of the store. "I thought I caught a glimpse of some—"

"Wait," Ben interrupted. His flashlight beam glinted against something to the rear of the electronics store. It shifted into shadow. "Is that—"

Shots rang out. With each one, the firing pin lit up a figure behind the gun.

"Down!" Ben yelled as he collapsed against a shocked Ruth. They slammed into a display of radio-controlled helicopters, then squirmed for cover along an endcap.

"Lincoln!" Morgan screamed from across the way. "Get down before—!"

"Dammit!" Lincoln cursed, blood spattering from his bicep before he fell. Morgan pulled him to cover along another display.

"Lincoln?" Ruth bellowed over more gunfire keeping them pinned into position. She pushed Ben aside and his back slammed along the metal shelving. He clutched tight to her wrist, locking her with him as a bullet whizzed down the aisle.

"Ruth, don't!"

"Talk to me, Linc," she continued, unafraid, unaware of the nutcase's position. Her only concern seemed to be for the man across the store.

"He's fine, Ruth," Morgan answered. "I've got him. Take care of this clown!"

"It's just my damn arm," Lincoln seethed. "I'm good."

"Ruth…" Ben said, trying to pull her attention back. More shots echoed, sporadic reminders of the threat.

"He's—"

"Morgan has him, Ruth. He's going to be okay. We're all okay." Her eyes wavered. Dusty brown pupils faded to gray in the beam of the scattered flashlights. She shook them awake and Ben turned for the right wall. "Cover me?"

She nodded, letting out a breath. When the shots died down from the back she stood to fire high and away from the shooter. It was just enough for Ben to scurry down the three aisles for the end of the store.

Keeping close to the ground, Ben crept farther. Ruth's cover fire gave him breathing room, and he took it, using the tall display of bargain DVDs to block the shooter's view of his presence.

Peering between the racks, Ben found the man causing their current predicament—if man was the correct label. Mess was more appropriate. He shuffled along the open flooring in the back, a tattered white robe swirling around him as he frantically scanned each aisle. Slippers skidded along the tile, and his dark gray sweatpants were stained in various degrees along his thighs and knees. A thin beard covered his cheeks, his hair overgrown and tangled atop his sweating brow.

"Sir?" Ben called out. He crept toward the back. A shot snapped in his direction. Ruth responded with her own barrage, keeping the man occupied long enough for Ben to reach the cashier counter. "Put the gun down, sir! We are federal agents! We want to help. We're trying to find out what's happened—"

The top of the DVD display shattered, crashing over Ben's shaking body. He dropped his makeshift shield and dove for a nearby stack of printer boxes, one near his right foot taking the heat from a wide shot. Styrofoam exploded into the air.

Ruth stared at him from the edge of the endcap. She pointed to her right ear intently. "I don't think he's listening, Riley."

Ben read the look and nodded. He crouched less than ten feet from the back displays of the electronics store. Ruth laid down another wave of cover and Ben realized the reason behind the miscommunication.

The shooter was wearing headphones. A direct connection kept him confined to the back of the store, the cable jacked into one of the stereos resting on a series of shelves on the opposite side.

Other devices, including a number of computer terminals still up and running, dinged sporadically. Ben didn't recognize their purpose. They didn't matter, though, not with bullets flying. All he needed was a second to explain. Something the man refused to offer, fear rampant in his swollen eyes.

Ben took a sharp breath. "Screw this."

He stood and fired at the stereo bank across the store. Sparks flew as he emptied his clip into the unit.

"No!" the shooter yelled out as he fell to his knees in terror. He tapped the butt of his revolver against the headphone then ripped the apparatus from his head. Wheeling around to the now broken units, he panicked, trying to bring each to life, and in turn finding no success. "No, no, no, no…"

"Drop the weapon," Ben demanded, Ruger locked on the man. His steps were cautious, even with Ruth working her way from the front of the shop.

"I've got him," she noted.

Morgan nodded the same from her vantage. She stuck close to a quietly cursing Lincoln by her side.

"Why?" the man moaned. He raised the gun on the approaching agent. "Why would you do that?"

Ben kept his own weapon cocked and ready. "I only want to talk."

"I would have talked!" the man shouted. "If I had known. I… I couldn't be sure. Not after what happened. Not after he took it. But why would you do that?"

"The gun, sir," Ben repeated. "Drop the gun."

"It doesn't matter anyway," the man cried. The gun slipped from his hand.

Ben rushed to his side and kicked the pistol away, finally able to take a breath. "Why? Why doesn't it matter?"

"Don't you get it? Don't you see?"

"See what?"

The man turned to the shattered stereo units and the dead headphones. Tears streaked his cheeks as panicked eyes locked on Ben. "You just killed me."

CHAPTER SEVENTEEN

Ben paced silently along the back of the store and waited. Bottles lined the wall leading to the office and beyond it the chain and padlock that had kept them from entering from multiple vantage points. A case of water and energy drinks made up one pile. The other was better left to the imagination, although the smell confirmed his suspicion.

Their shooter sat in a metal chair placed in the center of the open floor space. He ran his hands along stained sweatpants, unable to keep from fidgeting. The tattered robe was white, and not a robe at all upon closer inspection. It was, in fact, a labcoat, though rag would have been a more-apt description.

Surveying the store, Ben located the breaker panel and switched on the neighboring circuits to the one labeled STEREO DISPLAY. A thin row of lights flickered then held. The man in the chair shielded his swollen eyes from the sudden illumination.

No thanks came from the others. They were wrapped in discussion down the center aisle of the store. Any hope of meshing well out of the gate was a lost cause. If Ben hadn't been distracting Ruth with his inane sarcasm she might have seen the shooter sooner. Hell, he might have as well.

"Sit down," Ruth demanded, hand tight to Lincoln's shoulder. Morgan struggled to clean his open wound. Crimson ran down his bicep.

"I'll handle this guy, Ruth," Lincoln snapped. "I know exactly how to handle him."

"Just what we need," Morgan grumbled.

"Dressing him up as a patient isn't the answer, Morgan."

"Neither is shooting him," she argued. She tapped his arm and he pulled back in agony, holding back a scream. "Haven't you figured that out yet?"

Ruth shook her head, then stepped away with Morgan in tow. Ben kept his distance. He circled the scene and the man at the center of their current predicament.

"How is Lincoln?"

"Bullet went through," Morgan replied. "Bleeding has slowed, or rather it would if he would stop moving so damn much. He'll live."

Ruth rested heavily on a nearby display. Her hand covered her brow and her eyes snapped shut for a long moment.

"How are you doing, Ruth?"

"Fine." She pushed past Morgan for the waiting medical kit, supplies scattered along the floor of the store. "Just need some aspirin."

Morgan pointed to the cut along her arm, caked blood pinning her coat to the wound. "I can take a look if you'd —"

"Aspirin," Ruth repeated.

"Bottom left. Small pocket in front."

"Great."

Morgan held her hands to her hip, hesitant to speak. Ruth retrieved the pills and downed three in one gulp. She tucked the bottle into her pocket and left Morgan to her patient.

"Enough of this," Lincoln announced. He swiped the sweat from his brow and struggled for his feet. "I'm not going to sit here and —"

"He's not well," Morgan muttered, blocking his path. "Whatever is happening here might be affecting this man too."

"Let it."

"Shut the hell up, Linc," Ruth ordered. "Morgan?"

"I'll take care of the wound."

"Good." Ruth turned toward the seated man, surprised to see Ben already there. "Riley?"

Ben kept his focus on the shooter. He handed him a bottle of water. The ragged figure snapped open the bottle and took a long sip. "I figured we'd start with some simple questions."

"Riley," Lincoln shouted. "Let me handle —"

"It's fine," Ruth said in a calming tone. "Let him, Linc. Give him a chance."

Ben smiled at the support, then continued, "I'm Ben. And you are —?"

The man, satisfied at his drink, let out a long breath. "Thank you."

"You're welcome, mister —?"

"Doctor."

"Ah," Ben said. "Apologies for not recognizing your title. I didn't notice your diploma stapled to your forehead. Yet it still doesn't quite answer my question."

"Clevinger. Howard Clevinger."

"You're a rarity in Bellbrook, Doctor Clevinger. Care to explain why that is?"

"Lucky," the doctor answered quickly. "Just lucky, I guess. Or was, anyway."

"How long have you been holed up here?"

He surveyed the bottles in the corner and took a long whiff of his dingy undershirt beneath the labcoat. "Four days. More or less."

Ben shivered. "I'd pick a place with a shower next time. Maybe pack a change of clothes too."

"There wasn't time!" Clevinger yelled, rising from his chair. Ruth raised her sidearm at the sudden movement. Her thin eyes studied the man's intentions carefully. Clevinger's panic faded and he collapsed along the chair once more. "Not much sleep, you know?"

Ben wiped the sweat along his brow. "Energy drinks might not have been the best choice. Maybe some warm milk next time?"

"Needed them to keep the sugar rush. Glucose in the bloodstream may play a role. Played a role..."

"In what?" Ruth asked, finger tapping lightly along the hilt of her weapon.

Clevinger shook his head, eyes to the floor and his ratty slippers. Ben crouched close. "Where is everyone, Clevinger?"

"Doctor."

Ruth took a step closer. "When you explain what your degree is in you'll get the title back. How about that?"

Ben shook his head. Antagonizing the suspect would only go so far. This man was on the edge. He needed a helping hand back. "I get it, I do. We're trying to understand what happened — what is happening — here."

The doctor clamped down on the armrests of the chair, and his lips pursed — refusing to open to the line of questions. Ben felt the daggers coming from his colleagues. Pushing for answers wasn't working. He needed a new approach.

Ben rounded the chair once more, examining the man. Deep scars ran along the back of his hands. Numbers etched in his flesh from a long time ago. There was a 2 on one hand and an 8 on the other.

"Tell me about the scars. They look painful. Did you cut yourself?"

"No."

"Why these numbers?" the agent pressed. "28? 82?"

"28."

"Why 28?"

Clevinger tucked his hands into his pockets, refusing to meet Ben's questioning gaze. Instead, he focused on Ruth down the aisle. "Biology. My degree is in biology."

Ruth continued to roll her finger. "Fantastic."

"Doctor, please," Ben said. "We want to help. Where is everyone?"

"Gone," he answered. "Just gone."

"But not you? Why?"

"I was here."

"You mean you broke in here," Ruth commented, pointing to the shattered window.

"I had to," Clevinger responded. "There wasn't time."

"It's okay, Doctor. No one is going to blame you for that. However, we need to know: why only you?"

"I tried," he said, hands frantically tapping along the chair. "I tried to tell them. Tried to make them see what was coming, but they…"

"Tell us."

"You know already!"

Ben lowered his voice to calm the panicked man. "Doctor."

Clevinger pinched the bridge of his nose and closed his swollen eyes. "They vanished. Small numbers at first. A block here. A neighborhood there. Peggy, the store manager, I thought she was still here. She wasn't. Even the kids. Everyone."

"Where did they go?"

"Exactly!" he exclaimed. "I asked. I did. When it was reports and randomness. Only it never is, is it? No one cared. About any of it. Neighbors. Friends. Even family. People simply gone and no one, not even the police, could be bothered. It was in their eyes. You could see it in their eyes, you know?"

Ben didn't. He had no clue what the man was telling them. All he could read was the terror in every word and the fear in his voice. "You said you knew what was happening."

"I... I recognized it," Clevinger said, unable to peer directly at the questioning agent. "From my work. Migratory patterns based on biological triggers—environmental, systemic, and chemical. This was different."

"You found the signal," Ruth said.

Clevinger's eyes sparked with recognition. "Constantly moving, but always broadcasting. With its presence, people changed. Eruption of emotion followed by silence. I wanted to leave, but I could feel it. Inside. Started to hear it. Every movement, every beat, right in—"

"You said moving."

"I did, yes."

"You've been tracking it?"

His gaze lowered, then it turned to the shattered displays along the wall. "I was."

Ben shook his head. "But you're not affected."

"I was, then I wasn't. Now, thanks to you...?"

"I didn't know," Ben said—not only to the doctor but also to the irritated Ruth Heller.

Clevinger reached for the headphones on the floor. He lifted them to his ear before dropping them once more. "Hair band rock. Mid to late 80s. Blocked the noise."

He continued to mutter and Ben left him to it for a time. Ruth waited nearby and the two leaned close, eyes always locked on the man.

"You believing any of this?" The question left his lips and he wondered if he had his own answer.

"He knows what happened, but he's hiding more than a little something."

"Agreed. What though?"

Ruth shook her head. "From what I can see of the equipment he jerry-rigged, he definitely appeared to be tracking something."

"Look," Ben started. "I didn't—"

"Enough new guy," Lincoln interjected from down the aisle. "Finish the song and dance with this yahoo."

Ben nodded. "All right, Doctor Clevinger. Where is it now?"

"What?" the man asked, terror rising. "You can't. I mean, you can, but proximity might be a factor and your exposure…"

"We're fine. Or so I've been told. Now where—?"

Clevinger jumped to his feet. He pushed Ben aside and rushed for the front of the store. Ruth reached out to stop him, though her hand fell away at Ben's silent insistence. Morgan and Lincoln followed suit and all stuck close to the staggered steps of the man in slippers.

"It's stationary," Clevinger said as he stepped out of the store. "It has been for the last twenty-four hours."

"Where?"

Rain began to drip from the heavens, the clouds above gray and dark. Clevinger pointed west. "Where do you think?"

All turned to face the vast forest looming at the edge of town.

CHAPTER EIGHTEEN

Coffee spilled from the lip of Zac Modine's cup, catching him along the wrist. The steaming liquid pooled along the counter as he reached for a towel. He dabbed his hand before wiping the counter clean. His fingers paused at the end, hovering beside the washbin of stored cups used by the staff. Most brought their own and left them at their desk. Some simply forgot about them after a long day. One, however, was displayed prominently—never to be forgotten.

Grissom's cup.

It read #1 *Secret Agent* on the label in bright bold lettering. There were mock bullet holes in the background that were mirrored on the opposite side. Grissom had always held tight to the mug, mingling in the break room with the staffers and researchers rather than sitting in his office.

Zac rubbed at his eyes and turned away. Exhaustion was catching up with him. He wasn't surprised. Three days on shift with nothing more than a six-hour rest in the living quarters on the fourth floor offered him little recharge time. The extra shifts weren't mandatory. No, this was on him and only him.

He took another swing at drinking some coffee and met with success. The dark brew seared his insides down to his gut. He leaned against the counter and savored the sip.

The break room of the DSA held dozens of tables and chairs, but few occupied the space. Most of the staff remained at their stations to pick away at the constant flow of work. It was the nature of the agency. A catch-all related to more than the work itself, but to the people employed in the warehouse in Bethesda. Employees housed within had been given a second chance to make something of their lives.

Zac saw it time and again with recruitment. Those in need, those wishing to continue after an error in judgment or a mistake out of their control, were brought in over others hoping to play the typical politics that inhabited every government bureaucracy from the post office to the White House. Right or left didn't matter. The DSA stood above that and asked for the same in return.

Scanning the room for the ideal spot, Zac spotted Stephanie Atwater. She sipped her tea, book in hand, focused on the written word before her. Zac strode over and sat beside her.

Stephanie closed her book. She lifted her mug and he did the same. "You know this can't last," she said with a smile.

As the words left her lips the door to the room slammed open. Metcalf entered, heels clacking against the laminate.

Zac head sank. "You said it, not me."

Stephanie stood and straightened her skirt. "Director? How can I—?"

"I came for Zac." He shot up, wiping at a dribble of coffee from his chin. "If you have a second, that is?"

"Yeah," he replied. He put his cup down, hesitated for a moment, then picked it up again. The contents ran over the lip and down his fingers. "Of course."

Stephanie sat, a smile on her face as she opened her book.

"Lucky," he whispered before following Metcalf for the door.

"I usually am."

Metcalf led him into the hall and around the corner. The dull roar from the bullpen at the heart of the first level dipped into the background.

Zac finished his coffee, careful to keep from spilling any further. "What can I—?"

"There certainly seems to be a buzz in the air this evening," Greg Sullivan said. He followed their movements around the corner. Metcalf's eyes flared hot before she tempered them with a grin at his arrival. Sullivan ran a hand through his beard. "Anything going on I should know about? Or the Council?"

"Just another day in paradise, Greg," Metcalf quickly responded. "I was just about to go over some routine protocols with Zac, if you'd like to join us."

"Routine? Pass," Sullivan said. He tucked his hands deep into his pockets and started down the hall. "I've had my fill today.

Think I'll head home for the night."

"See you tomorrow."

Sullivan nodded without looking. Metcalf waited until he was near the exit, then motioned for her office. They stepped inside, the door clicking shut behind him.

"You *did* tell him about the Bellbrook operation, right?"

Her eyes thinned. "Have you traced the server used to give us the case?"

Zac ran a hand along the back of his neck. "I've tried. Whoever did it is good. They've covered their tracks well."

"So that would be a no."

"Well, yeah, but—"

"Then no, I haven't told the Inter-Agency's lapdog about our illegal operation in Bellbrook."

"Illegal?" he exclaimed. "I didn't realize I—"

"Nothing will be put on you, Zac," Metcalf said. "I was the one who made the call."

"But why?"

"This is a chance to show the Council how useful we can be— how with a few more resources, more agents at our disposal, we can be a fully functional force within the system."

"If Sullivan finds out though…"

Metcalf cut him off with a cold stare. "He won't."

"Okay," Zac said, unsure. *So much for the DSA being immune to politics.* "So what can I do for you?"

"I need two things," she answered. "You won't like either one, but you're going to do them."

"Is this about the team? Has something happened?" It had been eight hours since the team went silent—the moment they crossed into Bellbrook. Eight hours of waiting with no word as to whether or not the team was still alive. As to whether or not a threat even existed. They had no intel of any kind. Zac hated that feeling more than anything.

"Still no word," Metcalf reconfirmed. "Not what this is about though. I need some files secured. My eyes only."

Zac's brow furrowed. "Command-level clearance allows you to lock any directory you—"

"Not secure enough." Metcalf lowered her voice. "Can you make it happen?"

"Sure, but I don't know why—"

"Second request," she said, her voice quiet and her hand on the door to make sure it stayed closed. "I need you to track Sullivan. Full digital footprint, on and off our system. Call logs. Everything."

"Susan—"

"Director." She took a breath. "Zac, I need you to do this."

"He's deputy director. He just got here and you're treating him—"

"Zac. He's been digging through my files. Through directories he has no right to—"

"Have you talked to him?" She offered no response, and his head fell to his chest. "Right. Above my pay grade."

Her look softened. "I'm not condemning the man. I just don't trust him yet."

"Well, spying on him should help build that bridge."

"A precaution, nothing more."

Zac nodded. "Like securing the files."

Metcalf pulled out a small piece of paper and handed it to him. "These are the directories."

He read the file paths and immediately handed the note back. Metcalf tore the scrap three times over before allowing it to find its new home in the trash can tucked next to her desk.

"Thank you." She opened the door and he shuffled for the hall.

Zac found no words. There was no understanding Metcalf's actions or desires. Only his loyalty to the work mattered—what should matter to them all. Still, her decision irked him. Combined with the arrival of a new field agent without any advance warning, it felt as if he had been dismissed as a common grunt instead of a critical component in the department. The idea, the very thought, burned in his veins, threatening to explode. "Director, I really think—"

"I'll be in Operations soon."

The door shut in his face, drowning out his unspoken request. He stared deep into the metal slab for a long moment while he waited for it to open again.

"Right," Zac grumbled in surrender. "I guess I'll head there now."

CHAPTER NINETEEN

"I'm not condemning the man. I just don't trust him yet."

Metcalf's conversation with Zac came through the earpiece with crystal-clear clarity. Even over the pulsing traffic rushing out of the DC area, Sullivan picked up every nuance, every inflection of the director's voice as if she were seated across from him in the town car.

His driver shot him curious looks, to which he replied by raising the glass divider. This wasn't to be shared, hence the small speaker resting in his left ear. This was for him alone.

"Bellbrook…" The name settled on his lips as the echo of Metcalf's door resounded in his ear. He removed the earpiece and sank deeper into his seat, a smile on his lips. There was a reason behind the rapid movement of personnel at the warehouse, one purposely hidden from him. Now he knew why and he also knew what he could do with the information.

Outside, the city slept with its eyes wide open. Pedestrians wandered the streets, the decent temperatures quickly diminishing with the fading sunlight. Cars blitzed from block to block, caught in an endless loop of traffic. All were oblivious to the truth around them, to the work being done behind closed doors.

Work which controlled every aspect of their pathetically insignificant lives—a level of control now within Sullivan's grasp.

His phone rang, stirring him from his pleasant rumination. "Yes?"

"You sound pleased with yourself, Greg," the voice said, deep and hoarse. It fit Donald Stallworth, Assistant Director of the National Security Agency, perfectly.

"I am, Donald. Long night?"

Stallworth huffed. "I didn't call for conversation. She took the bait?"

Rummaging through her files was meant to be loud. It was meant to be seen and acted upon. Metcalf's fear, her suspicious attitude toward his clumsy attempt to view sensitive documents, surprised him though. He'd always assumed she was smarter than that, at least enough to realize a ploy when one was dangled before her, instead of jumping in whole hog.

"She did."

"This is dangerous, Greg. There are easier ways to get the information when her guard is down."

Sullivan shook his head to no one. "The woman's guard *doesn't* come down. But raise her suspicions? Make her paranoid enough and she will make a mistake. In fact, I believe she already has. Tell me, Donald, does the Council have any current operations in Bellbrook?"

"Bellbrook?" Typing fingers answered him. Deep breaths boomed in the speaker. "Ohio? Not a one. Why? Has something—?"

"I'm looking into it now," Sullivan said.

"Greg, if they find out what you've been doing—"

"What *we've* been doing, you mean," Sullivan interrupted. "Don't you trust me anymore, Donald?"

"She came too close to our operation in Buffalo."

"She found nothing and the damage was mitigated," Sullivan lied. Riley's recruitment had been unforeseen. Did they know more than they were letting on? He decided not to share that question with the figure on the other end of the line. Not yet.

"This is a dangerous game we're playing. If the Trust should learn of this betrayal? You need to be aware of the risks."

"I am. And I am handling it as I see fit. That is why they put me at the DSA in the first place, is it not?"

Stallworth had made the motion to the Council. None had complained. None had found fault. Frankly, the position didn't deserve the argument. Metcalf ran the DSA and anyone else was second fiddle, barely worth their notice. That was his hope in the appointment. He was the wolf in the fold—waiting for the sheep to slip from their pen.

Waiting to pounce.

"The Wellspring?"

"Buffalo was a misstep, one that will not be repeated. The Wellspring will be ours. All in good time." Sullivan hung up the phone before Stallworth could comment further. His hand rustled along his beard. He let out a thin breath. The leather of the plush interior cushioned him like a body pillow.

An operation in Bellbrook without proper authorization? One hidden from not only him but the Council? Metcalf played her own dangerous game, and it was going to catch up with her faster than she could possibly imagine.

Sullivan scrolled through the contacts listed in his phone and selected the appropriate number. It rang loudly twice before a voice greeted him.

"Yes, dear. I need to speak with General Adams about a situation developing in Ohio. Tell him it's a *trusted* friend."

CHAPTER TWENTY

Water pooled in Ruth's hands, the rain increasing with each passing breath. Filled, she splashed the cool, clear liquid over her face. Her hands held firm to her cheeks, then ran up through short-cut locks.

Closing her eyes helped. The effect, however, diminished with each attempt. Her body fought against her wishes, struggling to betray her with each step. Her head pounded and her muscles ached. The cut on her arm pulsed, deep red caked under her thin jacket.

It had been a long day, the flight and drive here not expected when she'd crawled into the office from another late night. Another perfect night, but one she denied occurred in the presence of the others. She was field leader now, promoted due to the loss of Grissom. This was their first mission under her command and she was fading fast. Heat billowed from her chest. Her eyes wavered, unable to focus on anything or anyone.

Aspirin did little to curb the effects. Her third dose in two hours caused her stomach to begin to cramp up. The three round pills joined her breakfast along the far side of their SUV.

Ruth watched the contents of her stomach flow to the nearby sewer grate, and she found herself wishing she could join them in the dark. She was tired and exhausted; the thought of making decisions was nauseating, though it was a better solution than relying on others.

Especially Lincoln. He fought every choice, every order given. His attitude threatened to fray the team, something she refused to let happen. She owed it to Grissom to keep them in line, to continue the tradition he'd set forth during his tenure. She owed him so much more, but it was all she had to offer the man who had given her a second chance.

Ruth opened her eyes. The moon was tucked behind the clouds. Streetlights provided the only illumination along the dark Bellbrook streets. The forest loomed in the distance, menacing from afar. What secrets it held needed to be known. They had to find the source of the signal. That was the job, no matter the illness she felt. No matter her fear.

No matter how much she disliked the idea of spending another minute with Ben Riley.

"This might not be the smart play," he said, rounding the car. Ruth shot up at his approach. She quickly wiped away the drool on her bottom lip.

"It isn't," she said. A deep breath filled her and agony swelled in her chest. Then she turned to face the recruit. His smile unnerved her, his naiveté at their situation. *Who the hell is this guy and what was Metcalf thinking bringing him on the team?*

"Okay," Ben held the word out as Morgan joined them. "So let's not drive into the ominous forest to find a mystery signal that is making people go whack-a-doo before pulling a Houdini?"

Lincoln glanced at her from the storefront window, constantly keeping the pacing form of Howard Clevinger in sight. His dark eyes were heavy as he judged her reaction to Ben's stupidly efficient summation of their situation.

It made her want to scream. Or was that the pounding against her skull? Her fists balled up tight to her sides. Before she could respond, Morgan stepped forward.

"Go easy on him, Ruth."

"I have been," she snapped through her clenched jaw.

"What?" Ben asked, a chuckle escaping. "Wait. Is this because I saved our butts back there?"

Ruth pushed through the pain. Her finger prodded the man's chest. "You mean how you shot to hell our best chance at figuring out the exact position this signal was coming from? How you took it upon yourself to open fire without any knowledge of the equipment you were ruining? Yeah, Riley, this is about you and that idiotic move."

"Well, you're welcome."

Fingers clutched tight to his jacket. "And you're a pain in

the—"

"Ruth!" Morgan pulled her off Ben, then shoved her against the side of the SUV. Morgan let go, but the exhausted woman hung close to the cool exterior of the vehicle, letting it soothe the raging inferno growing inside. She shouldn't have lost it. Ben had stopped a shooter and put an end to an unknown threat. None of them could have done better, but she couldn't bring herself to say it aloud.

They needed that equipment, not the word of Howard Clevinger, to put an end to the threat in the forest. They needed a chance to understand what was coming, what was waiting for them in the dark. Walking into the unknown was what had taken Grissom from them.

Ruth closed her eyes, letting the darkness take over. She was in charge, yet control slipped from her as easily as her breakfast along the rain-slicked parking lot. It was never a job she'd wanted; she had been content with the tech side of each mission using skills learned from her time at the NSA. She succeeded through knowledge. Unfortunately, all they had in Bellbrook were questions. They needed answers, not only for the sake of seven thousand residents.

But for their own lives.

"Ruth, listen…" Ben started, but she just shook her head.

"Just get in the car," she exhaled and opened her eyes.

"I can drive."

Ruth held out the keys to him, then pulled them back. "Like hell you can."

Ben laughed and returned to the other side of the vehicle. Lincoln flipped him the bird before returning to his task.

Ruth reached for the door, but was stopped by the worried expression spread across Morgan's face.

"You sure everything is all right with you?" Morgan asked.

Ruth's head drooped. She pulled her soaked hair from her forehead and nodded. "I'm fine."

"That cut—"

"Is just a cut. It's no big deal."

Morgan's arms crossed her chest, cocked eyebrow questioning her resolve. Ruth turned toward the electronics store. Lincoln rested against a nearby display, gun in hand. It was how she always pictured him when she closed her eyes. That and his smile, the one few ever saw on the job. One he shared with her.

"How is he?" she asked, her voice soft against the raging wind. "I mean, how is he really?"

"Lincoln? He's all right," Morgan replied. "What about the good doctor in there?"

"He knows more than he's saying. Way more."

"So ask him?"

"Might have to do more than ask, Morgan."

The medic of the team took a step back, ready to argue. She was always ready to argue when it came back to the violence of their job. Ruth reached for her shoulder and squeezed lightly, eyes catching the tall woman's deep, brown orbs.

"Hey," she breathed. "We need to know what he's hiding."

"Right."

"We'll send word as soon as the signal's down. Keep your comms open."

"Make it quick, all right?"

Ruth huffed then reached for the door handle.

"And maybe don't kill him yet."

She shot Morgan a look of disbelief. "Like him that much?"

Morgan shrugged. "Not really."

"I'll do my best," Ruth laughed.

She slipped behind the steering wheel. The key turned in the ignition and the engine drowned out the rain for a moment before the storm surged back. She flicked the wipers on, letting the windshield clear for a second. The forest filled her view.

Ben reached for the radio, but she slapped his hand away on instinct. They didn't need the symphony of static as background noise to their travels.

Ruth sighed and shifted the SUV into drive. "Let's get this over with."

CHAPTER TWENTY-ONE

"They on their way?"

Lincoln's question pulled Morgan from the street. Their rental turned the corner, tires squealing as they picked up speed for their destination. The rain followed suit. A full blown storm soaked the area. Wind whipped Morgan's hair from her face, chilling her to the bone.

Or was it the chill from the look in Ruth's eyes that cemented that feeling? Eyes of quiet desperation pleaded for assistance that would never be truly accepted. Morgan had wanted to call her back—if only the moment had held for a second longer. If only she could have found a way to make it right, to have made the correct gesture to win Ruth over from her stubbornness. She hoped she would have another opportunity.

"Yeah," she said. She shifted from the rain back into the shop. Glass cracked under her flats. Her smile offset the sickening sensation deep in her gut. "I don't think they'll be picking out curtains anytime soon."

A grin curled from the corner of his lip, though Lincoln did his best to suppress the emotion. His focus remained on the third member of their party. Clevinger paced across the back of the shop; his tattered robe billowed behind him like a cape. His slippers tripped him up, but he failed to care as he muttered notes under heavy breath.

Lincoln lowered his sidearm, aggravated as Clevinger began another lap. He settled against a support column in the shop. "Warn him about Ruth's driving?"

"The keep-your-head-down-and-your-mouth-shut lecture?"

"That's the one."

Morgan shrugged. "He'll figure it out."

"Cold."

"With reason," Morgan said.

Lincoln's brow furrowed. "Riley?"

"No," she answered, holding the word for a second too long. Something about their new colleague set her off. Perhaps it was the fact that Metcalf had never consulted the team in the first place. Maybe it had more to do with Metcalf recruiting at all. Grissom had run the team, part of his role as deputy director. Grissom had come with too many memories, too many emotions—and too many regrets. Just like Ruth's pleading eyes. "Not Riley. Him."

Clevinger was an oddity. Out of everyone that had been trapped in Bellbrook when the signal began, somehow he'd survived. Not only survived, but taken steps to save himself over all others. He understood more about what happened than he shared—they all recognized it in his hesitation. In the answers that weren't said more than the ones offered to the team.

She groaned, pulling her hair back and tying it off. Mysteries were one thing, but this was something else, something she wanted no part of. This was bigger than them, bigger than she could understand, or wanted to understand.

Turning away from Clevinger, she focused on Lincoln instead. He refused to say anything, but his pained glances made his condition clear. Morgan opened her pack and called him over with a fresh bandage dangling between her fingers.

"Still can't believe he shot me," Lincoln said. She tore the bandage away, and his jaw clenched tight at the act. He shook his head. "A damn nutjob in a labcoat."

"Never an apologetic cheerleader with a nursing degree."

They shared the laugh. Quietly, Morgan pulled his shirt away from the wound. A deep scar ran along the skin. Lincoln refused to catch her sadness, locked on the good doctor, locked on anything but her reaction. He snatched the bandage away and tore the adhesive from the backside before slapping it in place.

"How long has it been?" Morgan asked, adjusting his shoddy work.

Lincoln's fingers grazed the scar as his shirt settled into position. "Not long enough."

"Afghanistan?"

"No."

His answers were curt and all she'd expected. They had both served. Her role as a medic had brought too many mistakes, ones she refused to admit let alone mention to any of the others.

Lincoln remained a soldier through and through. He served a mission—much like the one given by the DSA—not people. People betrayed each other. People came with agendas. They served themselves over all others. No platitudes. No sacrifice. None interested Lincoln. He swore to something greater: a flag, an ideal.

He served something that couldn't die—something that would never fall to irrelevancy.

Lincoln's eyes wavered, softening slightly. "Sorry, it's just..."

"Never apologize to me, Linc. We both saw our share of horrors."

"Yeah. Yeah we did." He laid his pistol across his lap. "You know, when the Taliban shot at you, you understood it. Here? Away from war, away from desperation and fear of death every second of every day? Nothing makes any damn sense."

"War is hell."

Lincoln shook his head. "Surviving is hell. And that's all we've ever done. Ruth doesn't understand. After what happened with Grissom though..."

His words trailed off and he let them fall away. The moment faded, but she held on for a second chance. "Want to talk about it?" Morgan shifted closer, her voice low. "About Ruth? You two seem—"

Lincoln stood, pain wracking his face. "We good here?"

The wall closed between them. The same one she held for others. It was better in the long run—safer. For the sake of the mission, if nothing else. Every tragedy was held under their tongues, swallowed hard with each gulp of air. The distance allowed them to function in society, allowed them to laugh and love with everyone else.

Surviving was hell. But it was all they knew how to do.

"We're good," Morgan replied. She stood beside him, hand reaching then falling away. She let the moment slip away as easily as Ruth's flimsy excuse.

Lincoln pointed to their company. "I can handle him if you'd like." Her eyebrow cocked and he rolled his eyes. "Without the gun, if necessary."

She started for the waiting doctor. "I've got it."

They needed answers. More than recrimination, and more than remembrance, they needed to know the secrets surrounding Bellbrook. Only one man held them. There was no getting around it. It was time for Howard Clevinger to start sharing with the class.

CHAPTER TWENTY-TWO

The SUV swerved to the left. Rain blotted out the dim light offered by the flashes of lightning splitting the clouds overhead. Ruth cursed, swinging the rental back to the right side of the road. Her pace never slowed. Her thick boot pressed harder on the accelerator to maintain their momentum.

Before them, the forest loomed.

Ben couldn't look. Staring at his loafers, he wondered if he would ever have the opportunity to buy a pair that fit. His curiosity took him from the simple black pair two sizes too small to the idea of his new apartment. He knew nothing of the place, and the others were not forthcoming on much, let alone their own residence in Bethesda. Was it furnished? How was the view? Simple questions served as easy distractions keeping the weary agent focused on anything but the road ahead.

And Ruth's driving.

Music helped, or would have if the radio was functional and he had been allowed to utilize it. Instead, *The Power of Love* blasted in his head, and visions of Marty McFly skateboarding across town drowned out the reality of their journey. Playing with his tie also helped matters, but the approaching trees played havoc with any notion of calm.

"I don't mind driving," Ben announced. Ruth stared straight, teeth grinding at the sound of his voice.

Sweat pooled at the base of her hair, down her neck and cheeks. Her skin, not exactly smooth and elegant to start, grew more pale the closer they came to the forest. Sharp eyes of brown flickered to gray, glazed over and lost. She was fading and said nothing, betrayed nothing in the quiet pain that slipped out with every breath.

Ben tried to help, tried to find a way in. He recognized the anguish. She was in more pain than she cared to admit, the same as his father had been at the end. Always pushing away from help, always willing to grin and bear it even when everything begged for a reprieve. He had failed with his father. He didn't want to do the same with Ruth. Yet every attempt was rebuked. Every kind word was assailed. Every joke lost to silence.

There was no winning her over.

It was the same with the others. Lincoln hated him at first sight, possibly over his concern for Ruth, which stood in Ben's thoughts as simply ludicrous. Morgan wasn't much better, if indifference could be called an improvement. Ben's presence brought up issues and memories yet to be dealt with.

He'd taken the job, promised Metcalf to give it a try, but if he was the only one willing to show up how much of a chance could he take? He wanted to make a difference—to see the world changed for the better. How could he though, blocked by stubbornness and a team unwilling to offer anything of themselves? He didn't have an answer of any kind to the questions plaguing him. So, Ben did the only he could when he ran out of answers.

He kept talking.

"Really," he said, smile plastered and voice growing to match the rain outside. "I drove every day on the job. Working the beat, just like you said. Okay, maybe not every day. Emily, my partner, preferred to be behind the wheel, but every once in a while she let me take a stab at it. Okay, every once in a while might be a stretch. Really it was only once, and only for a block before she—"

The SUV screeched to a halt. The rain battered the exterior of the vehicle, a troubled beat in the background. Ben sat back, the trees surrounding them behind the storm.

"Let me stop you there," Ruth snapped. "Check your gun, say a prayer, I don't give a crap. I'm not, I repeat, I am *not* bonding with you right now."

"I see," Ben replied.

Ruth let out a low breath and hit the gas once more. They weaved around curves in the road. Large bends dominated the path through the extensive forest. Ben held his tongue for a long moment, hands clasped against his knees. Then he turned to face her once more. "I can still ask why not, right?"

Ruth refused to stop, eyes ever forward. "I'm busy trying to keep us alive."

Ben settled against the headrest. "Ah."

"What?" Ruth yelled. The car skirted to the left-hand side of the road. She jerked the wheel to bring the swerving vehicle back before it left the pavement completely. "Just what, Riley?"

"Nothing," he shot back. "No, I get it. This is about the shoes I'm filling. That's what this *crap on the new guy attitude* has been, hasn't it?"

"I don't know what you're talking about."

"What was his name?" Ben recalled the plaque in the basement of the DSA warehouse. He followed each and every member of the team, including those stuck in Bethesda pushing paperwork. It hung over them all, from the empty seat around the briefing room table to the dusty coffee mug in the break room. He had mattered to them and continued to do so, to the point where all newcomers caught nothing but distaste and anger. Rather than meet their feelings and tackle their grief, they had laid it at his feet. "Say it, Ruth. Just say the man's name if he meant so much to you."

"Grissom, all right?" Her hand slammed against the steering wheel. A lone tear mixed with the sweat down her cheek. "His name was Grissom and you'd be lucky to fill *one* of his shoes let alone the pair."

Ben pointed to the loafers scrunching his toes. "Probably a better fit than mine, that's for sure." A thin glare shot his way. "Hey, I get it."

Grissom's shadow covered everything related to the DSA — from Operations to Logistics to Research. Ben was nothing more than a stranger. That had to change. If they ever made it out of Bellbrook, that is.

"So what happened?" Ben asked.

"We should almost be there, Riley. Why don't you — ?" Ruth's hands slipped from the wheel, rising to meet her temples. She screamed. Nails cracked pale skin and drops of blood flowed along her thin fingers.

"RUTH!" Ben grabbed the wheel to keep them in the lane. Ruth's foot pressed down harder on the accelerator. The momentum shot them forward into the darkness. They left the road during the first curve, mud from the storm spraying across the side. "Ruth, come on. Keep it together."

Her hands fell away. Gray eyes faded to white and then sparked to a dim brown. "What the hell—?"

"Thank God."

She knocked his hand away and took the wheel, guiding them back to the center of the winding strip of interstate. "Dammit, Riley. What were you—?"

He came out of nowhere. A man stood in the middle of the road, short and thin, with round lenses covering his eyes.

The rain made it almost impossible to see, the wipers flapping back and forth vigorously in their efforts to help. Ben reached for the wheel and spun hard right. Ruth, attention trapped on the figure before them, joined his efforts.

The SUV swerved. Tires left the safety of the rain-soaked pavement. The vehicle toppled to its side, then continued rolling along the road. Sparks flew, windows shattered within. Ignoring the screams of the pair inside, the Suburban careened forward, upended completely in the effort, and crashed headlong into a thick oak at the edge of the forest.

There were no more screams.

Only silence.

CHAPTER TWENTY-THREE

Darkness surrounded Ben. Arms dangled below him, hands caught in the shattered glass coating the ground. He couldn't see, couldn't breathe. They'd crashed. He remembered that much. The SUV had tumbled over, sending him reeling across the passenger side. There was a deep-rooted fear in Ruth's face. It was more than just the sparks flying around them and the windows shattering along their laps and cutting into their flesh.

It was a fear of an uncontrollable end.

Ben stirred. He fought against the safety harness strapping him in place. He slapped at the release, the smallest amount of pressure causing great waves of pain to rise from his palms. Droplets of crimson pooled along his fingertips. They spread around the cab with his flailing movements.

Suddenly, the buckle dislodged and Ben fell to the roof of the upended car. He cried out, shards of glass slicing along his arms. His scraped hands protected his face to the best of their ability. Shuffling along the glass, Ben worked his way to his knees. Rain flooded into the cab, cooling the sting from the myriad cuts decorating his skin.

Ruth didn't move. Her eyes remained locked shut in the driver's seat as her weary frame dangled over him. A moan escaped her lips, agony deeper than any crash. Ben tried to reach for her, crying out with each inch while glass crunched beneath his shifting.

The smell of gas had yet to present itself, though the rain may have muddled the effect. Ben refused to take the chance.

"Come on, Ruth," Ben muttered. He reached for her belt release. Ruth's hand jutted out and snatched his wrist, squeezing tight. Her eyes snapped open. Her pupils had faded to white.

"Don't you hear that sound?" she screamed. Then she collapsed, her head lolling around limply.

Ben let out a deep breath. "Let's not do that again please. This day has been enough of a nightmare."

The release clicked and the pale woman's body dropped into his waiting arms. Ben bit his lip hard to swallow the pain. He kicked out at the frame of the door, which buckled easily thanks to the crash. It smashed out, allowing flickers of moonlight into the glass-ridden cab.

"Come on, Ruth," he whispered. Her moans carried through the swirling wind, muffling his struggles to pry her loose from the SUV. Her leg caught on the mangled car door. She cried out as a sharp plastic protrusion dug into her skin. A stream of blood smeared along the ground behind their escape.

"Dammit," Ben cursed. Quickly and without as much care as he would have liked, he placed Ruth on the other side of the tree that served as the final resting place of their vehicle. He propped her against the thick trunk of the tall oak. The remaining headlight gave him something to work with, a stream of white to survey her injuries.

The cut on her right leg was at least four inches long. Thick streaks of dark blood spread through her pants. Ben applied pressure to the open wound. His hand immediately sent a shockwave through Ruth's body that caused her to slam her head against the trunk of the tree.

Her scream tormented him, but he refused to relent. Her eyes sparked, dusty brown filling the center.

"How?" she tried to shout, but it came out as a whisper lost to the storm.

"I've got you," Ben said. He pulled his tie loose with his free hand.

She rubbed the back of her head, wincing at the touch. When she caught sight of his hand on her leg and the blood running down the sides despite his efforts, she stopped.

"How bad?"

"No dancing for awhile. Sorry."

Ruth let out a short chuckle, the effort turning to a cough. Her stubbornness made Ben feel worse. The cold, gruff exterior she wore like a badge of armor soothed him more than the fear that sparked from that simple laugh.

He lifted her leg carefully and slid his tie beneath. Her jaw tightened and she sucked in short, shallow breaths in preparation. "I heard you like that tie."

"It'll grow on you."

Her hand fell on his, scared eyes wide. "Tell me."

"It's bad, Ruth."

She nodded. "Tell me when you—"

"Now." Ben pulled the makeshift tourniquet tight along the wound. A sharp cry rose over the clapping thunder, leaves shaking overhead from the sound. The stream slowed to a trickle, at least for the moment.

Time hadn't been on their side since their arrival in Bellbrook. Now it made a play to be their worst enemy, one Ben couldn't beat. Not so far away from town, and certainly not alone.

Ruth trailed his gaze, concern growing. "What is it? Riley, what—?"

"Keep pressure on the wound," he said. He guided her hand to the gash. She squeezed, stifling terror and pain.

"Where are you going?"

"There was someone on the road," Ben said, picturing the figure that had caused their accident. His black suit and hat. The rounded spectacles were opaque, rather than clear, and covered his eyes. "Are you—?"

"Go," she answered.

"I'll be—"

"Just go, Riley." She closed her eyes and pressed down on the wound.

Ben broke out in a full run. He circled the wreck of their car, slipping through the mud for the slick pavement of the road. It curved in both directions. The path through the forest continued for a mile in either direction.

His staggered steps carried him to the center, and his eyes squinted through the downpour. Lightning cracked the night sky, shining a light on the street. There had been a man standing there—almost waiting for their arrival.

He smiled at us.

Now he was gone. They were alone, without a means to call for backup or a way to inform their colleagues of their situation.

The signal, locked deep within the forest, blocked everything.

What was the right choice? What was the correct path? Either option put Ruth at risk. Her wound needed attention from a medical professional—if Morgan could be called that. She was, however, the best qualified to try and stitch up the broken woman. Even if she received treatment, there was no way to know if it would truly help Ruth. Her agony stemmed from more than the crash.

The signal ended one threat. Medical care took care of the other. Neither path aided both.

Ben raced back to his patient, hands in agony as they swiped at the rain coating his skin. Ruth's grimace faded at his approach.

"Anything?" she asked, a ray of hope shattered at his gaze.

"Nothing," he said. "I could have sworn—"

"I saw him too."

He rolled up his sleeves, letting the rain wash out his cuts. His arms wrapped around her to lift her from the mud-soaked earth, then he stopped.

"You sure you're okay?"

"Besides my leg being split open like a hot dog bun?"

He grinned at her irritation. That was the Ruth he had come to understand over the course of the past day. The sound that she had yet to completely throw in the towel. The one that offered him a chance to make things right.

His fingers ran lightly along the back of her head and down her neck. "Are you sure? Nothing with your head? Your shoulder?"

"No," she snapped. "Nothing. What the hell are you—?"

His fingers grazed her shoulder. They were coated in deep red, the fading light of the crashed SUV catching the color.

"Blood?" she said. Her hand left her leg on instinct. It ran the length of her shoulder and trailed down her back. "I don't—"

Ben stopped her and returned her hand to her leg. He stood, hand catching the flow at her shoulder then following it up and away from Ruth.

"What is it?" she asked, panic in her voice. "Ben, what do you see?"

He didn't know how to answer, didn't know if he *should* answer. He picked away at the cracked bark of the tree and the flow increased, thick and dark. He pulled his hand away and showed the injured woman as crimson dripped from his fingertips.

"The tree," he said, staring at his hand. "I think the tree is bleeding."

CHAPTER TWENTY-FOUR

"Signals. We are bombarded by them. Radio waves. Cell phones. Television. Wi-Fi. That dull hum in the back of your mind helping you fall asleep so you don't realize how alone you truly are in this world. They can be so much more, however. Manipulation—both behavioral and emotional. This one strikes on a physiological level."

Morgan paced in front of Clevinger as the shabby scientist in the ragged labcoat took a pause for a drink of water. He finished his third bottle of the last hour and tossed it aside to join the mound of emptied containers accumulated during his stay at the electronics store. He opened the fourth immediately.

Lincoln held back, nursing his arm when he thought no one was looking. More was bothering him, but Morgan let the subject lie. She noticed small things, like the sweat beaded along his tight-cropped hair and how hard he leaned against the support beam, but she hesitated to discuss them with the wounded agent. The arguments with Ruth had served as enough of a warning to keep her silence on the subject. Arguments were not necessary. Only answers. That was where she hoped Clevinger led the pair—though with each passing ramble doubt crept across her face.

"Impossible?" He caught her glare. "Your eyes scream it. Let me guess... a medical doctor?"

Morgan stopped and shared a glance with Lincoln.

"Don't bother answering," Clevinger continued. He dropped the water beside the chair, then gripped the armrests to steady himself. "It doesn't matter. The human genome, you see, is malleable—flexible. It changes with our conditions over time. Vast amounts of time in most cases. However, it can be instantaneous with a secondary trigger involved."

He lifted the bottle of water once more and held it out. Morgan continued to circle around the back of the shop, shaking her head at the offer.

"Smart girl," he admitted. "Might be viral. Of course there *is* the chance it's airborne. Possibly a food source. Milk, bread, eggs: something universal to the population. A vitamin, perhaps? It comes back to our DNA as nothing more than a tool to be used."

She followed his wild eyes as they sought out something more, some other thread to follow. They sparked and faded under the dim lights of the shop, and they appeared to be unable to focus on any one object. The good doctor seemed unable to grasp reality, at all.

Leaning close, Morgan heard Lincoln's concern in the form of a grunt. She waved him back, unconcerned as she approached the seated subject. In fact, she smiled at both her colleague and the sweating lump in the chair.

"Someone is awfully chatty all of a sudden, don't you think?"

"I have threatened to shoot him," Lincoln said with a shrug. "Repeatedly."

Morgan nodded. "I think there's more to it."

She leaned in, but then almost fell back from the heat rising from his odorous frame. His skin was milky white, caked in sweat despite the bitter breeze blowing from the shattered front window.

Clevinger stomped his foot. "It's changing this town, Agent! The signal—"

"How far along are you?" she asked, ignoring his ranting. "Sweaty palms—"

"Headache. Outbursts," he snapped. He returned to the chair. He sank in the cushion like a man lost. "I'm aware."

Morgan shared the sentiment. June, the clerk from the convenience store, had displayed similar traits. Ruth as well, though Morgan hoped they meant something different. It was a fading hope, but one nonetheless.

"How much longer, then?"

"I don't know!" He jumped at her. She reeled, kicking away from the man. His hands remained locked on the armrests. His eyes bulged, fit to burst from their sockets.

A gun clicked in the background as Lincoln inched toward his target. The sound snapped something within the frantic doctor, who quickly settled down, his head low.

"I don't know."

Morgan approached once more, slower this time. "I have my medical kit. Antibiotics. They might block the symptoms."

"For a time," Clevinger said, his voice cracking. "The change will still come, though."

Morgan shook her head. "A physiological change? How can a damn signal do that?"

His eyes went cold. "Mankind is capable of anything."

"You think someone is doing this?" Lincoln challenged, gun tight in his hand as he propped himself up against some nearby shelves.

Clevinger read his disbelief warily, yet remained calm at the sight of the gun. "The moon landing. The atomic bomb. Both were seen as impossibilities at one time."

"You think someone is in that forest drawing people there?" Morgan tried to wrap her head around the man's ranting. Time slipped away from them. Every second wasted without answers, without knowing what they faced, put Ben and Ruth in danger. The town of Bellbrook counted on their intervention, and they had failed at every turn. She couldn't let that stand. Not again.

"Why?" Morgan pressed. "For what reason would someone do this? Here of all places? Mass kidnapping? Experimentation? If so, to what end?"

"Don't you get it?" Clevinger bellowed. "Don't you see? The forest!"

"The one we passed coming to Bellbrook?" Morgan confirmed.

"Yes. Exactly," Clevinger announced. "Thank you!"

The forest. Where Ben and Ruth were at that very moment, hopefully putting an end to the nightmare surrounding them all. She was tired of Bellbrook, and she could tell the same from the wounded soldier at her backside. She could tell that and much more about her suddenly silent colleague. Sweat pooled on Lincoln's skin. The color surrounding his wide pupils dulled to gray.

"What about it?" Lincoln asked.

The joy in Clevinger's eyes, the shared understanding, slipped to desperation and he let out a groaning sigh. His hands ran over his lips and trailed up to his bleary eyes. He stomped his feet in a panic.

"No, no, no," Clevinger muttered. "How can you not see? How can you not know?"

"Howard," Morgan said, her tone soft and comforting. Her hand rested on the man's, fighting the urge to pull her fingers back from the scar of the number two and the thick layer of grime covering his skin. "We need your help. What about the forest? What are you trying to tell us?"

He snatched her hand and pulled her close. His eyes screamed to be heard. "There is no forest."

"Let her go!" Lincoln shouted. "Do it now!"

"Howard, please listen to me," Morgan said. She struggled against the man's grip. He was stronger than he looked. Could it have been another symptom of the signal? Was he one step closer to whatever was at the end of the journey? "I want to help you. Let me help you."

"There is no —"

"It's right there!" Lincoln barked. He ripped Morgan free and shoved her aside in his anger. She rolled along the ground into a nearby display. The gun shook in Lincoln's hand and he pressed the barrel deep against the sweating man's forehead. "You sent Ruth there. You know it's there, so quit dicking around and tell us what the hell is going on!"

"Lincoln," Morgan called. She rested on her knees. Her hand reached out for the gun. Lincoln refused to look at her. She turned to Clevinger instead, hoping for another second. "Howard. What don't we know?"

"There is no —"

"Howard," she repeated, stronger and clearer than before. "You have to tell me. You have to give me something right now. What is it about that forest that has you so scared?"

Clevinger stared into the barrel of the gun, at the weapon threatening to end his life. His gaze held no fear —no desperate plea. His defiance dared Lincoln to pull the trigger. Silence swallowed the shop and Morgan closed her eyes, wishing it would end.

When she opened them, Clevinger turned to her and let out a

breath. "That forest?" he said, fighting through his pain, struggling through his own confusion.

He pointed toward the wilderness at the edge of Bellbrook. "That forest wasn't there a week ago."

CHAPTER TWENTY-FIVE

Operations was Zac's home away from home. Displays along the back wall, typically lit up with bio-readings, were blank thanks to the signal jamming all others within the small town in Ohio. Staff ran reports back and forth, maintaining the priorities set by Metcalf and the bullpen above. Work stations occupied the middle of the room for various members of the team. Communications. Logistics. Everything ran through Operations.

The left-hand corner served as Zac's office. A short cubicle wall offered him a modicum of privacy, one maintained by a large sign asking for all others to keep their distance when noticing him behind the computer screen and typing away. It wasn't a distance he wished to keep, merely a necessity to accomplish the work at hand — or so he told himself.

Especially this work. Zac closed his eyes as he collapsed in his chair. He ran his hands through his hair. He needed a donut — or ten. Complete and total sugar rush to dilute the sense of betrayal offered by one boss for another.

Sullivan was new. Appointed by the Council directly, he came from the world of politics, bringing three decades of opinions and agendas with him. Zac understood Metcalf's reticence when it came to trust. The DSA stood for something better. To spy on his movements though?

Zac ignored the thought and logged into the system. His wife's picture briefly smiled at him as he keyed in the memorized information. Files ran the length of the screen, blocking Claire from view. Hundreds of reports and images were locked in a series of directories he never heard of let alone noticed within the confines of their server.

"What the hell is the Wellspring?" he muttered as he worked. The secure key directive initiated and he quickly input the encryption key, cycling to the sixteenth digit before finalizing. He jotted the selection of letters and numbers down and ripped the note free from the pad. The paper slid inside his pocket, and he patted it lightly before continuing.

Sullivan's system sprang up on the console. Emails, reports, files, and photos. The man's personal collection of phone numbers alone was extensive, though Zac wished he wouldn't keep them so visible and easily found by unwanted visitors. Zac uploaded the monitor program, then paused. Before he could initialize it, a shadow spread across the desk.

"Something just popped up on radar out of the Chesapeake," a petite brunette said, her voice nervous at approaching his domain.

"What?" he asked. He ended the monitoring program without initializing it, then turned off his screen. He stepped around the cubicle wall and joined her on the main floor with two other staffers. All looked at the display map tracking two objects over Maryland airspace. "What the hell are those?"

"They're moving fast, whatever they are," one said.

"No indication of origin? No flight plan logged in through the tracker?"

"Can't be commercial," the brunette said.

"Get me confirmation. Check satellite feeds, anything that can tell us what they are."

He didn't say it out loud. Refused to entertain the very idea, though he knew exactly where the objects were headed without question.

They were moving straight toward Bellbrook.

Zac reached for the phone near the door. Stephanie answered after a single ring, though he cut her off immediately. "I need the director down here. Now."

CHAPTER TWENTY-SIX

Ben lumbered deeper into the forest. His shoes stuck in the muddied earth. The weight of his colleague bogged down their momentum just as much as the relentless rain. The trees did their best for cover, the branches thickening and snapping above as they made their way along the ridge; the town of Bellbrook was no longer in sight. Even with the growing canopy overhead, the rain soaked through their thin jackets and chilled their very bones.

Ruth's pain grew with each breath. The agony swelled along her head, fingernails drenched in blood as they pierced her temple to quiet the growing cacophony in her skull. Her screams did little to help Ben's own suffering. He trudged along without a sound.

The cut in her leg aggravated their progress. His tie was drenched in the center by thick blood, constantly flowing like the rain above. Ben thought the forest was the safer route; he believed it to be the faster path back to Bellbrook, where Morgan might be able to aid Ruth's injuries more than his lackluster effort.

Each step, each cry from his companion, undermined that thought. Bellbrook remained out of reach, out of sight. It was lost to the growing forest that surrounded them on all sides.

"Riley," Ruth cried as she slipped from his shoulder to the soft earth.

He reached for her hand, but she knocked him aside, her eyes crooked and crazed. "We can do this, Ruth."

"Just stop," she said, exasperated. "Please just stop."

"Stop what?"

She pointed back to the road, back to some semblance of sanity. No mention was made of the bleeding tree, or of what it meant to their search for the townsfolk of Bellbrook. Or what it meant to Ruth's growing pain.

"Head back. Get Morgan. Tell Lincoln —"

"*We* can do that," Ben said over the rain, his hand little more than a wiper along his soaked face. "Together."

"No," she answered, shaking her head. "You can."

"I'm not leaving you."

"I am giving you an order!" Her hands collapsed along her temples, squeezing tight to her skull for relief.

Ben crouched next to her. "I regretfully refuse to follow it, then."

She batted his efforts back until finally he looped his hands under her arms and pulled her to her feet. Shuffling beside her, he lifted her left arm over his shoulder and resumed their journey through the forest. Both noted the growing limbs, stretching between the trees above like a great yawn. The trunks thickened and layers of bark spread down to the ground.

"You can't carry me the whole way," Ruth muttered.

"Won't have to. The signal. It has to be around here. You said so yourself."

She shook her head. "It's dark, and the storm is not letting up. The forest is larger than we imagined and my leg —"

"Will be fine."

"Ben," she called. "My head —"

"Is fine!" Ben snapped. He stopped, turning to her with a soft smile and saddened eyes. "That is a direct quote by the way."

"Don't remind me."

Through the rushing wind and the crack of lightning, Ben paused. Fifty yards down the ridge he spotted a small break in the trees. He pointed, excitedly, and the strain of carrying his passenger and the pain running along his cut hands and arms disappeared.

"There's a clearing up ahead," Ben said, pulling her along. "Could mean we're close. We can at least get our bearings, try to see how close we are to town and —"

"The road was safer."

"Yeah, well, it added a mile to the trek. You can make the decision next time, promise."

He trudged ahead, her feet shuffling through the growing muck from the storm. The signal had to come from somewhere close. He just needed time — time enough to save Ruth and make the difference he hoped to make with his decision to join the DSA.

"I wonder..." Ruth said. "I wonder if Grissom could feel it too. His time, I mean."

"Knock it off."

"You asked what happened," she continued, eyes shut from the world. "It's what always happens with agents at the DSA. We shouldn't have been there, but we were. I made a choice, passed the buck instead of owning the decision, and he paid the price. It was my fault, Riley. I should have helped him, fought for him more." She stopped, planting her tired feet into the earth. It forced Ben to halt at the precipice of the clearing. "But this? Ben, this isn't on you. You've done enough, you hear me?"

He shook his head. "Keep moving."

"How?" she yelled as she dropped to her knees. "How can you be so frustrating?"

He let her rest, searching the area for signs of life. Some indication they had come to the right place — that his choice was justified. Instead of answers, instead of the clearing offering the absolute truth about what happened to the people of Bellbrook, there was emptiness.

"No," he whispered. "It can't be like this. Not after everything..."

Ruth fought to breathe. "Ben. You have to keep going."

"I thought for sure..." he said. All hope departed the small opening in the deep forest. He started for her once more, refusing to let another moment pass. "Come on. We can—"

She screamed, hands against her head.

"Ruth!"

Her eyes pleaded with him. Her tears mixed with the sweat and rain running along stark white skin. Gray pupils faded to white. "Ben," she moaned. "I need... I need you to do something for me."

"What are you—?"

She reached to her hip and drew her weapon. She held it out for him. "I can't... You don't know how this feels. That sound, that awful sound in my head. I can't do this, Ben."

"No," he said, moving away. "Not going to happen."

Her hand shook and the gun fell between them. "Please, Ben. I can't—"

"Neither can I!" he shouted over the crack of lightning splitting the sky. "I won't!"

"Ben..."

"We can do this, Ruth. We can reach the others and figure this out."

She fell away, collapsing against the earth. Ben grabbed for her, though her body was too heavy, too exhausted to assist in the effort. Not that she wanted to anymore.

"Please, Ruth, let me save you. I have to—"

"She doubts you can."

Ben spun around, sidearm cocked and leveled on the new voice echoing around them. Across the treeline, stepping into full view, stood a short, lithe figure all in black. He wore a dark fedora and thick round lenses, blocking his eyes from view. His smile, however, widened with each step into the clearing.

"I do as well."

CHAPTER TWENTY-SEVEN

"You can't be serious."

Lincoln's words echoed in Morgan's thoughts. Clevinger's pronouncement, the secret that the forest had not existed one week earlier, staggered the pair. His words gave Morgan pause. To him it was the truth, but to her—due to her medical background, a place that demanded to be grounded in humanity—everything screamed in contradiction. She fought his truth to the core of her being.

She couldn't though. "You have a better explanation?"

They inched toward the front of the store. The pounding rain muffled their voices from the frantic doctor unable to sit still. Lincoln winced as his arms crossed his chest. "A better explanation than the people of Bellbrook turning into trees? Give me a minute and I can think of a dozen."

Morgan waited, drawing a glare from the tired soldier. "I don't like it any more than you do."

"That makes me feel better, at least."

"I think he's on the level though," she added. "About this, anyway."

Something bothered her, however. For as long as they had been with Clevinger, for as long as they had been forced to listen to his rambling, every revelation had been held back, arriving slow like a steady stream. The most important question of all remained. How had a signal like that come to be? Who could put something like that together, out of sight from an overbearing government with non-stop regulations to stymie that type of research in the first place?

Morgan almost didn't want the answer. She sure as hell knew

Lincoln wanted nothing to do with it either. He struggled with the work in that regard. Because of his reticence, his inability to see the broader picture when it came to the science behind the crimes they investigated, most at the DSA believed him to be nothing but a mindless thug—an ex-soldier demanding a target without remorse or conscience.

He was anything but. Morgan noticed in the way he'd reached out to Ruth earlier, in the concern he shared with her in questioning Clevinger. Time and time again in their relationship the most humanity, the most loyalty came from his silence. Always present, always willing to be there, no matter the cost.

"What's the play?" Lincoln leaned on the support beam near a display of high-definition monitors. Sweat puddled along his crew cut and down his neck. "Hope Ruth and the newb find the nutso behind this?"

"Lincoln?" Morgan stepped closer and waved her hand in front of his eyes.

"What? What is it?"

"You tell me," she said. "When did it start?"

"When did what—?"

"The fever," Morgan snapped, unwilling to waste time. "You're sweating."

"I was shot."

"Yeah, and the meds should be helping." She grabbed her bag. "Knock off the macho bull and be straight with me."

"It's nothing," Lincoln said, his bloodshot eyes unsteady. "This isn't going to help anybody."

"You don't know that," Morgan said. "If Ben and Ruth can find the signal—"

"They have to," Clevinger declared. Both turned to meet his manic gaze. He staggered along the center aisle of the shop, knocking over boxes of goods never to be purchased. "This... this isn't the first town."

"What?" Lincoln asked.

"Spring Hill, Kansas," Clevinger continued. "Six months ago. It's gone now. Forgotten. Just like we will be."

"How?" Morgan's question was strained. She reached for more, trying to make sense. How could it have happened before and no one knew? How could a town disappear without even one news story or one headline, let alone hundreds, about an event of that magnitude? How did something like that happen and become lost to the world?

Clevinger ran his hands over his face. Sweat dripped like rain from his fingertips. "It was an accident the first time." His head tilted to the side, and a sad smile formed on his face. "I barely escaped with my life. But this?

"I don't know how he found me. I thought I had taken the necessary precautions. I should have smashed the device. I burned his notes, but I couldn't destroy it. He found me. He took the prototype and activated the signal."

Clevinger staggered toward her, his skin white as a ghost. "You have to stop him. This is all my fault, but I can't, I'm not… You have to be the one."

"Morgan," Lincoln called. He raised his sidearm. "Back up."

"No, Lincoln," Morgan said. "We have to help him!"

"You can't," Clevinger said. "Not me. Not any of them. DNA is malleable, but only to a point. A change like this? They may as well be bodies in a mass grave."

Morgan shook her head, unwilling to accept his conclusion. Seven thousand people gone just like that? "No. Doctor, surely you're—"

"I watched it happen to Spring Hill," Clevinger raged. Spit flew with his words, and his hands clenched like claws as he continued to approach them. "It's my fault. I opened the door. I thought… I hoped I was helping. I thought I was creating something to save people—to save the future. That's what he told me it would be. Now it's too late. I can feel it inside. The anger. The lack of control. And then the emptiness. I won't let it happen. Not to me."

"Howard," Morgan pleaded. "Don't do this. It doesn't have to end like this. Please, Howard—"

Clevinger screamed, curling over in complete and total agony. His fingers dug into his skin, and peeled layers back like the rind of an orange in an effort to end the pain. His eyes widened and he launched at the agents. His bloodcurdling scream echoed around the store, and Morgan tripped backward, running into a waiting Lincoln MacKenzie.

"Down, Morgan! Now!"

"No!"

Three shots rang out and hit their mark. All three slammed

into Clevinger's chest. The first did little, the man's eyes lost to white. The second staggered him, and the third caused him to fall. His descent knocked aside twin displays and sent boxes scattering across the aisles.

Morgan sat, shattered and shocked. "Why? Why the hell did you do that?"

Lincoln tucked his sidearm away. "You know why."

She hated the fact that she did. Life mattered; it was what she stood for, her ultimate mandate—even in someone as dubious as Clevinger, someone who in the throes of death admitted to being the cause of so much pain and destruction in the small town of Bellbrook. Tears slipped down her cheeks and she wiped them away. Time for grief, time for regret, would come later. Ruth and Ben needed them. Morgan crawled over to the fresh corpse. She rummaged through the various pockets of his labcoat.

"What are you doing?"

"You heard him," she said, continuing her search.

"I wish I hadn't."

"Me too." She stood. A set of keys dangled from her hand.

"What's this?"

She clicked the alarm and heard a beep ring out. After helping Lincoln to the parking lot, she hit the button again and a sedan at the front of a nearby row lit up. She held the keys out to him.

"Here."

"Where are—?"

"Head east, away from the forest. The signal should cut out at the city limits." His eyes wavered over the keys and her directions. She stopped, following his gaze. "Lincoln? Can you drive?"

"I'm good," he said, clutching the keys tight. Her questioning look remained and he pushed past it. "I've got this."

"When you're out of the zone call it in." She opened the door to the sedan. "We need to contain this as quickly as possible."

"What are you going to do?" He caught her arm before she shifted for another parked car. "Hey."

"Lincoln—"

"You can't go in there."

She ignored him, testing the lock of the next car. Finding it wouldn't open, she moved on to the next. She had success on the third attempt. The door was unlocked and the keys remained in the ignition. Jumping inside, Morgan turned the key and the engine clicked over, roaring even louder than the thunder overhead.

Lincoln slammed a hand on the hood, leaning in the window. "Morgan, this is crazy."

"Crazy is what we do today."

"You have no idea—"

"I know," Morgan said. She stared down the road at the forest looming in the distance. The great forest and the danger within begged for her to turn away, to race in the other direction and never look back. Ruth and Ben were there, however, leaving no real choice in the matter. "But I have to try."

CHAPTER TWENTY-EIGHT

The wheel jerked under his grip. Lincoln struggled to keep the sluggish sedan straight as sweat poured into his eyes. His arm ached, the pain medication all but worn off.

He shouldn't have left. The team needed him. Ruth needed him. Running off with Ben of all people, the greenest agent he'd ever served with, was a fool move no experienced team leader would have made.

He should have been the one with her.

Lincoln blinked hard, the lights flickering overhead. The interstate curved and the thrumming of the rumble strip eased him back to the center of the lane. Peeling away from the main drag, the sedan circled left, winding a long ramp around a cliff at the edge of town. For Lincoln, the world spun. The last twelve hours were a blur of pain and confusion. Hell, the last month had been the same — the team continuing to tailspin from the loss of Grissom.

Lincoln knew more than he cared to admit about the subject. When he had lost his charge in the Secret Service, when the bottom had dropped out and he'd realized how little his existence mattered despite his dedication, the muted soldier fell hard.

Most days he was still falling.

Lincoln slammed on the brake. The road ended, gravel giving way to a small bluff overlooking the city of Bellbrook. He clicked the lights off and opened the door. His heart raced, his arteries threatening to burst through his neck. He took shallow breaths — too many, too quickly. His legs gave way and he collapsed along the side of the car.

How did it happen? When did the signal take hold of his

body? Was it the gunshot wound? Could it have been as simple as an open wound in an infection zone? Or was it more than that? Did it relate to their time spent in Bellbrook or possibly his own anxieties over the situation?

He closed his eyes, hands locking them shut. Beyond the car, a deer raced off into the night. Lincoln wanted to join it. Panic. Emotional outbursts. They were symptoms of a larger disease. So was a fever, and his forehead burned at the touch.

"I'm infected," he muttered, trying to come to grips with his situation. His hands squeezed against his temples and he screamed in pain. Every fear, every terror held from childhood flew from him. "I'm infected!"

Multiple tours overseas had done little to prepare him for the eventual end. All his time in the military, his days in the service of his country, taught him was to kill, how to take a life — the soldier over the man. The weapon over the hero. Howard Clevinger was merely the latest in a long line of victims at the other end of his Glock. Lincoln was nothing more than a killer.

I've earned this end.

He burned with fever. The world spun and his head pounded. He fought the pain, stared at his agony through the rain threatening to wash him from the cliffside. The thrumming in his head brought his terror home. The point of no return. The team relayed the store clerk's final moments before going stark-raving mad on them, and he witnessed Clevinger's first hand. Both had heard a noise, a godforsaken sound threatening to blow out their eardrums.

Now he heard it as well.

The sound rang out under the crashing thunder and the pouring rain. The ringing started to chime louder.

"Beth… One…"

Lincoln blinked. The noise wasn't random. It wasn't a signal or a sound.

It was a voice.

"Beth… One to… Ac…"

Lincoln's chest heaved and he raced around the car. Climbing the short cliff, hoping to get altitude, he clutched tight to his radio. The comm unit chirped at his side. The sound offered him peace compared to the panic of only moments earlier.

The meds were working. The pain was subsiding. The sound

was not the end. It was a lifeline, the crackling sound of a miracle in the form of Zac Modine's voice.

"Bethesda One to Team Actual. This is Bethesda One, do you copy?"

Lincoln laughed. At the top of the hill, the WELCOME TO BELLBROOK sign beside him, Lincoln wiped away his terror and his fate with a booming laugh.

"Lincoln?"

He tapped the radio to confirm. "Damn good to hear your voice, Modine."

"Thank God. Lincoln, we've been trying to contact you for over an hour."

"Been busy," the exhausted agent replied. Taillights flashed in the distance—Morgan's ride into the forest. She hauled ass but still had a way to go to reach the rest of the team. He should have been the one, not Morgan.

"Listen, Modine…"

"Lincoln, there isn't—"

"Modine," Lincoln snapped through the line. "I've been shot and people might be turning into trees."

"What? Lincoln, are you okay?"

"Yeah, that's a fair question to ask, but there's no time. We need containment. There's a possible contagion here and we don't have time to—"

"Exactly," Zac said.

Lincoln pulled the radio close. "What?"

"You have to get out. Right now. This very second. We're getting interference, so the signal is still in place, but if you're out of range of it then keep moving and don't look back."

"Can't."

"This isn't a joke, Lincoln."

"I'm aware," Lincoln said. "The team is still inside the limits."

Headlights rushed from the east. They were miles out, but barreled toward Bellbrook. Above the approaching caravan, twin lights in the sky burned brighter.

"How much time?"

"We're tracking inbound on your position, Lincoln. You—"

"I can see that, Modine. How much time do they have?"

"Lincoln," Metcalf said through the line. Her voice was calm and collected, stone cold against the raging storm. "You have fifteen minutes."

"Fifteen… That's not enough—"

"Fifteen minutes," she repeated, no emotion entering into the equation. "Then all hell breaks loose."

Their discussion continued, lost to the background. The taillights of Morgan's sedan slipped into the looming forest that hadn't existed a week ago. The last member of Lincoln's team disappeared from view.

Fifteen minutes to save them. And there wasn't a damn thing he could do.

CHAPTER TWENTY-NINE

It was the man from the road. Ben squinted through thick drops of rain at the black silhouette looming closer with each step.

The man's skin was rosy, at least what little Ben could see due to the black suit and hat covering him. The glasses didn't help. Instead of sharpening his features, they obscured his eyes. The lenses were opaque, not clear, though in the pale light there appeared to be a dim glow rising behind the round spectacles.

At his back, Ruth howled. She was curled into a ball, hands clenched tight to the gaping wound along her right leg. The pain was too much for her. Hell, it was too much for him to handle at this point, but there was no one left to stand for him, no one left to save the day.

If such a thing was even possible.

"Not another step!" Ben shouted across the clearing, the Ruger cool against his stinging cuts.

The figure continued to smile, the only feature Ben wished he couldn't view in the darkness surrounding the growing forest. Branches stretched in a large canopy to block the rain.

The man inched closer, hands at his side. One was opened and unarmed. The other, however, carried a small pen-shaped device with a glowing red light at the end and a dial along the side. His thumb hovered over the ominous button.

"Don't," Ben demanded. He leveled his sidearm on the stranger. "Stay where you are."

"Ben!" Ruth yelled, her eyes blank. "Ben, it hurts!"

He refused to turn away from the man in the clearing. "I know, Ruth. I need you to hang on though. Do you hear me?"

"I can't... Ben—"

"You have to, Ruth."

The man took another step forward. "You can make this stop."

"Who the hell are you?" Ben spat at the short, slender shadow of a man.

"Not someone to be questioned like a common thug." His words held razors behind them, each sharp and carefully displayed for Ben. The man in the suit stopped, sticking to the deep gloom created from the canopy above.

"Tough," Ben replied. "I'm holding the weapon."

"Are you now?" the man said. He depressed the red light slightly.

Ruth's agony increased. Her howling split the sky even more than the storm. The sound drove daggers through Ben's ears. Her pain was excruciating.

"That's enough," Ben said. The shadow's thumb held tight to the red light. Ben lowered his gun. "I said that's enough!"

The man nodded, accepting the offer. Ruth's cry diminished, and fell instead to a low moan. Her eyes remained locked on Ben, his stray glance enough to note the white filling the space completely.

"A name," Ben requested once more.

"Would do you no good," the man answered in a cold, deep voice. "I am nothing more than a witness to what this world will be. And what it has to be to survive what is coming."

Ben shook his head. "Gonna have to do better than that. I already met my raving lunatic quota for the day."

"Sanity is a matter of perspective," the Witness said with a wide grin. "I, however, am simply observant."

"Then look at the pain you're causing," Ben snapped. He pushed forward and the man eased back, his thumb close to the red light and in full view of the agent. "You can stop this. Tell me how."

"You surprise me."

"I surprise you?" Ben exclaimed. "I'm not the one playing God with the lives of seven thousand people."

"God has nothing to do with this," the Witness said. His empty hand grazed the thickening bark of a nearby tree. "Though the Garden is an inspiration. Most came peacefully, without pain or struggle. They arrived, ready for the change to come. Not you, though. You continue to stand, continue to fight to the last breath. Unafraid. Why aren't you afraid?"

"What are you—?" Ben's question fell short as the Witness depressed the button, locking the mechanism into position before shifting the dial to full. Ruth's agony joined his own as their screams echoed through Ben's brain.

Ben fell to his knees, hands covering his ears. His eyes squinted as he tried to maintain a focus on the approaching man. The piercing wail was no longer an external factor; instead it erupted inside his splitting skull. The contents of his stomach emptied in seconds, vomit spewing in deep hurls along the muddied earth. His body convulsed, legs tucked in close. He couldn't think, couldn't see straight.

The Witness knocked Ben's hand away from his ear. "Much better. You need to experience this. You need to feel it. It will make you better. For the future."

"Is that—" Ben choked, spitting the remnants from his stomach at the Witness' feet. His cries carried him from the mud, fighting through the pain raging beneath the surface to get to his knees. His chest heaved, his heart pounded, and his eyes wavered, but he refused to surrender. "Is that what this is? Some crap about destiny and the future? Making a name for yourself?"

"This?" the Witness said. "No. Consider this a simple test."

Ben shook his head. "You call the murder of an entire town a test?"

"Murder? I see no murder. I see... change. A change *they* have not anticipated, to be sure. One their so-called Wellspring could not conceive thanks to the ingenuity of Howard Clevinger. I planted a seed, and he supplied the garden. This is a change we will all wish for soon enough. I have seen what is coming. Do you know your place in it?"

"What the hell are you—?"

The Witness hovered over Ben. The red light burned in front of the young man's hazy eyes. "Listen to me and listen to me well. There is a reason you are here. A reason you have been chosen by them, your so-called DSA. You were too close to the truth in your past life. Too close to seeing the mechanism behind our lives. I am not your enemy. When this ends, when all this finally ends, I will be your only hope for survival. Remember that, Benjamin Riley."

How? How did the Witness know his name? About the DSA, an organization supposedly kept secret from everyone? Ben struggled to ask, struggled to do anything against the roaring red light of the signal device. The agony was too much for him, and he fell to his side. He closed his eyes to the world, wishing for an end, quick and merciful.

How much time passed, he couldn't say. The pain swelled through him for what felt like days, and then dissipated in an instant, carried away by the swirling wind in the clearing. Peace came with the solemn sound of dripping rain from the trees and the song of the first bird he could recall hearing since his arrival to Bellbrook. The cloud in his head lifted, and his eyes captured the world around him once more. Finding his feet, Ben surveyed the clearing.

The Witness was gone. His final taunts hung in the air—threats of a future unknown to all but him. His knowledge of Ben and the DSA raised the hairs on the back of the agent's neck.

There was no sign of his escape. No path left in the muddied earth. It was like he'd vanished from the scene.

"Ruth?" Ben called when he realized the silence of the clearing. "Ruth, are you—?"

He spun around to her position, the immediacy of their situation returning. If the pain in his head was gone now then it might have diminished for her as well. That still left the gaping wound along her right leg to handle. She needed treatment before she bled out, and there were miles to go before reaching help.

Ben stopped, his gaze crestfallen. Ruth no longer lay along the earth, hoping to be saved, hoping for something that would never come. In her place was a new addition to the great forest. It rose in the center of the once empty clearing.

"Ruth…"

Ben fell to his knees before the tree. In the thickening bark he noticed her eyes, the terror in her face. Only for an instant before they were gone; enveloped in the growing oak.

Resting in front of the trunk sat his tie. Ben cradled it in his hands. Next to the bloodstain inherited from his father's tour of duty was another splotch of crimson. Ben nodded, accepting the fact. Then he wrapped the tie around his neck and tightened it.

"From the job," he muttered. His father's words suddenly carried more relevance than ever.

A chirping split the silence of the forest. The rain settled in the background, and even the discomfort running along his hands dissipated behind the growing noise emanating from the tree that served as Ruth's final resting place.

Ben scurried around the trunk and found her radio lying among the roots. He pulled it close and held it to his ear.

"...da... signal... I say... Riley? Hel...? Come in, can you hear me?"

"Lincoln?" Ben asked into the radio. "Where are you? What's going on?"

"No time for your mouth, Riley. Just listen for a change," Lincoln said. "I need you two at the road. Morgan is en route. Move it now. Do you copy? There's..."

It took Ben a moment. The radio almost slipped from his palm as his colleague finished. "What? Lincoln, wait. Did you say air strike?"

CHAPTER THIRTY

Time was not on her side.

Light grew closer in the rearview mirror. The streaks along the clouds approached faster and faster. When they struck, their arrival would be enough to shatter the surrounding shadows and lay waste to anything that might be learned from this tragedy.

That was what it was, a tragedy. Seven thousand people were lost to what amounted to an accident. Science, mankind, where would the blame be laid? Would it fall squarely on the DSA for acting without thought, for rushing in blind for the sake of the mission?

None of this was what she'd signed up for. Death and loss were what she had run from after her fall from grace. Her secret mistake, the one that kept her from sleep, the one that pushed her forward without a thought regarding the footprints trailing behind.

It was that mistake that made the med-kit in the passenger seat a burden instead of bringing her the joy it once had. Her mother had given it to her—so proud of the woman her daughter had become. The whole family shared the sentiment.

Now she was alone.

The rusted-out Malibu sped ahead through the forest. The engine struggled, puttering along, but she kept the pressure up, forcing the neglected sedan to stay on the road. The trees towered on both sides. They looked so natural, yet their presence was anything but. They were designed, tested, and prodded like a great experiment. But for what reason? Why would anyone do this to the innocent? What had they stumbled upon?

DNA manipulation was cutting-edge science. It was light years ahead of anything being explored in labs throughout the world. At the moment, little more than theories on the subject existed. Even then, those researchers projected decades of study to determine the effects of such work. To cure illnesses and remove defective genes were workable goals: redeemable returns for years of study. But to take that research and use it in such a fashion?

Mankind is capable of anything.

That had been Clevinger's fear, but more than that—regret? Had he truly found a way to crack the code so easily and force the change on man? Plant and mammal on the surface stood as complete opposites, but studies showed similar traits embedded deep. Exploit those shared traits and what would be the result?

Morgan closed her eyes. The car took a bump in the road hard, causing the Malibu to shudder as it left the ground for a brief second. Too many questions plagued her, too many possibilities—each more impossible than the last. But then again, Clevinger had recognized her doubts, understood them as her training. She was unable to pierce beyond the physical to see his point of view. How could she? She wasn't wired that way.

Who the hell was?

Morgan opened her eyes and slammed on the brakes. The car reeled, struggling to stop. Brakes screeched, tires squealed, and the Malibu jerked back and forth. The engine fought to stay in place under the hood.

Trees surrounded her—growing, thickening with each passing second. Each one held a story. The entire history of Bellbrook was locked within the oak trunks spreading along the western border of town. So much life had been lost, all from an experiment gone horribly wrong.

From the corner of her eye, she noticed a figure step out of the forest. His tie whipped around his neck. His feet slid along the pavement. Ben looked like garbage, visibly hurt and near collapse from his experience.

Morgan put the car in reverse and turned around. As she sidled next to the fleeing agent she opened the passenger door, then tossed her medical kit to the backseat.

"Riley!"

Blood mixed with rain in streams down his cheeks, running

dark from his ears and all along his neck. "You heard?"

She didn't need the warning. It cracked through the air like thunder, streaks heading right for them across the night sky.

"Ruth?"

His chin fell to his chest and a hand over swollen eyes.

"Right," she said. She reached over him as he struggled with his seatbelt. After pulling the door shut, Morgan returned to the shifter and slammed it in drive.

The sedan soared back toward Bellbrook with its vacant streets and homes. Where seven thousand lives had ended without so much as a word spoken or a care given. And Ruth Heller. How could they have lost another so soon? How could she face Lincoln with that news?

The two soaring streaks dipped in the sky, dropping their precious cargo over the forest. Ben pointed at the growing lights, now doubled. Where the first continued on their trajectory, the second pair fell rapidly over them. The accelerator dipped to the floor, the engine roaring over the sound of the missiles crashing around them.

The world burned. Incredible explosions rocked the earth. The crashing of trees shattered the peace of the vacant town in Ohio. A wave of broken and burning oak covered the road, heading toward the fleeing vehicle.

"Morgan..."

"Hold on!" she yelled as light snapped in violent oranges and reds, the flames flickering to meet the beauty of the night sky. "Just hold on!"

The sedan screamed. Flames and the debris of the air strike rose to meet them. Their anger was only matched by the cries of the agents, hoping—praying—for one more second, one more inch of safety.

Hoping it would be enough.

The forest fell behind them, and the flames compounded as the jets made a second pass, dropping their payload on those lost to the world. Seven thousand victims met their fate, never to see another sunrise, never to understand the reason behind their transformation.

"Morgan," Ben called, eyes locked ahead.

"We made it."

"I wouldn't say that yet."

Six transports covered the road and blocked their escape. Twin camouflaged jeeps led the pack. The other four skidded to a halt beside Primrose Elementary.

"The military? Here?"

Morgan slammed on the brakes before meeting the blockade head on. Soldiers surrounded the car, weapons poised and ready.

CHAPTER THIRTY-ONE

The violent storm had nothing to do with the rolling thunder or the pouring rain. The growling came not from the engine of the borrowed sedan. The heat rising from the burning forest to their back held little more than a candle to that which rose within Morgan's breast.

And she was about to let it loose.

The car idled in the center of the road. Transports blocked their egress. The burning world at their backside locked them in place. Morgan's foot hovered over the accelerator, desperate for an opening.

Ben kept his distance. He held tight to the bloodstained tie around his neck, struggling with Ruth's loss and the story told by the man known only as the Witness. He wanted to share everything with the woman beside him in the hopes that their shared grief might in some way make up for the pain of their first mission together, cementing an artificial bond through some shared trauma.

He needed to feel that. He needed someone with him. Yet her cold stare pulled her further and further away. This wasn't his world. He didn't belong here. If there was someone in his stead, someone as heroic and steadfast as his predecessor, things would have been different. Perhaps Ruth might still be alive. Perhaps Bellbrook could have been saved.

Hate certainly would not be seething from Morgan's clenched jaw. Anger and rage would not be seeping from her bloodshot eyes.

"Morgan..." His call fell silent—unheard.

Behind the wall of soldiers and vehicles blocking their path more personnel departed the transports. They raced around trucks and removed equipment. Words were rarely shared, just efficient steps to resolve the problem at hand. Soldiers scattered to all sides. Four stopped short of the sedan and took aim at the two passengers within.

Morgan's hand left the wheel for her sidearm. Ben stopped her. "Don't."

Her eyes screamed at him, shaking his fingers loose from her arm.

"Morgan, don't do this."

"They killed her, Riley. Don't tell me what I should or shouldn't do."

She left the sidearm secured to her side, not even blinking at the weapons poised to end their time in the city of Bellbrook. Behind the armed guard surrounding them, a stocky gentleman exited the front jeep. He wore a brightly decorated uniform with stars along his broad shoulders.

The door to the driver's side opened before Ben could react. Morgan jumped from her seat for the pelting wind and rain. Ben reached for her too late, his words lost to the door slamming shut.

"Morgan, please."

By the time he left the sedan Morgan was already beyond the guard. Two of the four escorted her, weapons trained at all times. The other pair kept Ben company as he followed.

"What have you done?" Morgan bellowed. The stout soldier ignored her. Sharp orders sent those around him dashing in all directions. "Hey!"

He turned. His eyes, sharp like razors, hid behind bushy eyebrows of white. "Clear these people from the area!"

Morgan rushed the man, and hands immediately grabbed her from both sides. Ben tried to help, his weary limbs struggling to escape the tight grip of the well-rested soldiers. They raced around the grounds to gain control of the situation. One offered a report to his superior in the pinned stars. The name ADAMS adorned the general's chest.

"Perimeter secured around the forest, sir," the soldier saluted. "Checkpoints positioned on all sides."

"Excellent," Adams replied. "Send them in."

Dozens stepped from the cover of the caravan blockading the

road. They wore full-body suits and masks. Strapped to their backs were large tanks. A thick, insulated cable stretched from the bottom around and down their arm to a waiting trigger. A small flame ignited from the tip of the barrel of the extensive weapon.

Morgan's eyes flared as their flamethrowers came to life. Each started for the forest, adding to the destruction already wrought by the air strike. They razed the earth of something never before seen, something no one could know about.

"You can't!" she cried. She pushed and pulled from those locking her in position against the wet pavement. She kicked out, knocking one back. With the extra inch, she pounced up, and her head collided with the other's chin. Free from the pair she raced for the general.

"Morgan, wait!" Ben shouted, unable to move, unwilling to fight.

She stopped short of Adams. The surrounding soldiers cocked their weapons and aimed at her position. Her hands rose, struggling to tuck back the rage held within them for only a second.

"What are you doing?" she asked. She pointed to the forest. "Do you even know what this is? What you're doing to it?"

Adams puffed his chest. "Containing a potential threat, young lady."

He held out his hand and his subordinate approached. A tablet passed between them and he offered it to the waiting woman. She eyed it suspiciously, wiping the rain from its screen. "What's this?"

"Orders," Adams said. "Direct from the D.O.D. and the Office of the Secretary of Defense."

"The Department of Defense?" she muttered. She returned the documents without a second glance. "How?"

"We're handling it, Agent Dunleavy." Adams leaned close, a smug grin forming across his lips. "Let us do our job."

The flamethrowers blazed a clear path through the southeast corner of the forest, moving in multiple paths around the perimeter and through the center. They were methodical — unfeeling.

"You're killing them!" Morgan bellowed. Guns inched closer to cut her off from the general. "Listen to me. Just listen to me!"

"I have my orders."

"But you don't understand what this is," she continued. "*None* of us understands what this is, what it could mean!"

"Morgan!" Ben yelled. The men surrounding him let go, his hands open to minimize the threat. He reached for her, but she fought against his efforts.

A soldier exited their vehicle, his search complete. He shuffled through the contents of her medical bag.

"Don't you dare—" Morgan started before the armed figure removed the samples gathered at the convenience store during their altercation with June. He carefully placed them in a waiting container to the back of the closest jeep, then returned with the bag. Morgan snatched it from him, jaw clenched to match her fist.

Adams huffed at her anger, eyes reflecting the growing blaze despite the pouring rain. "Escort them to their colleague at the east checkpoint. I want this forest gone by sunrise."

"Like a damn memory," Morgan whispered.

"There's nothing we can do, Morgan," said Ben.

She shook her head. "No. There's just nothing you care to do. There's a difference."

She left him in the center of the road. Soldiers escorted her to a waiting transport, but Ben held back. The fires burned faster and higher with each tree caught in the path of the cleanup crew tasked with the destruction.

Each tree. Each person. The city of Bellbrook.

And Ruth Heller.

"That's not it, Morgan." Ben's fingers ran the length of his tie and the second splatter of blood marring the solid black of the fabric. There had been enough spilled tonight. He refused to add Morgan's to the growing pattern. "That's not it at all."

CHAPTER THIRTY-TWO
Three Days Later

Morgan strode through the ICU at Suburban Hospital in Bethesda, marking her third lap in the last hour, before finally stepping within the wing. Hospitals made her uneasy. Her history with them, in any and all forms, built up that tension and refused to abate, despite the years between being a practicing physician and whatever the hell she considered herself to be now.

A bouquet of daisies sat in her grip, the stems straining for release. Her nerves had little to do with the subject of her visitation to the anti-septic halls and more to do with the building itself. With each call, each code announced through the speakers, she walked faster. With each alert calling for assistance, with each crucial decision demanding to be made at a moment's notice, her nerves frayed.

When she reached his empty room, she realized the futility of her visit. Lincoln had never been the ideal patient. Hell, neither was she. After Bellbrook, however, she had hoped, almost prayed he would take the time necessary to heal from his injuries.

Morgan surveyed the halls, stopping at the building directory. Immediately recognizing her destination, she started down to the first floor, taking two steps at a time.

The rehab center was a well-organized gymnasium. Balance beams and matted floors made up the left side of the expansive space. On the right, fitness machines ran in long rows, ranging from top-of-the-line ellipticals to treadmills. Free weights were positioned along the wall. The entire rear of the room was a basketball court where staffers contributed in a friendly game in-between shifts.

Lincoln curled a forty-pound weight with his bandaged arm. Each rep was met with anguish in his eyes. The pained look vanished when he noticed her at the door.

Morgan approached slowly. "They gave you a room. You should use it."

"Been busy," Lincoln replied. He lowered the weight with a groan. She tossed him a towel, and he wiped the thick coating of sweat glommed to his skin. "Nothing on television anyway."

"You think you should be doing that?" Morgan stopped at the thin glare offered in response. They each dealt with the Bellbrook situation in their own way. She was no better, curled up on her couch while refusing to go into work, lost in her long-awaited book rather than face the reality they had witnessed. She wondered if she could ever face what happened, and knew, at some point, she would have no choice. Work was all she had left.

Lincoln joined her at the bench on the far side of the room, away from the rambunctious cheers of the basketball game.

She pointed to his arm. "How is it?"

"Fine," he muttered. "Arm's fine now."

"About Ruth…"

Lincoln shook his head. "Don't."

"Look," she pressed. "We lost Grissom. Now Ruth. It's a lot to take. I know. Metcalf does too. But you? You don't need to hide it anymore. About Ruth, I mean."

He hesitated, holding his words in check. He did a much better job than she had when she'd returned home from their mission. The first hours were lost to grief, the next batch thrown into a fit of rage. She was still deciding which way was healthier, which did her the most good.

Morgan stood and set the bouquet next to Lincoln. "Right. I just wanted to check on you."

She started for the door and paused at the sound of his voice. "I do get it, Morgan. What Ruth and I had was… well, it was what we needed. After losing Grissom the way we did? The choice we had to make…?"

"What happened wasn't on you, Linc."

Tears tucked back as he clenched his jaw tight. "It happened, and we've paid for it since. But don't… don't try and sell me on

Metcalf giving two seconds of grief over Ruth. Or Grissom. We've both seen the wall. Just another name, another body, all for the glory of the DSA."

"You don't believe that," Morgan said, hands to her hips. "You can't. Come on, Lincoln. We do the job. Metcalf and the rest? No matter where we started they respect the work."

"I used to think that. Now I see it for what it is. What we truly are." He stood, wiping his eyes with his towel. He dropped it and lifted the bouquet. "We failed the first time around. It marked us, our shortcomings and our mistakes. The ones always dogging our steps. The truth is that we need them. We need the job. It's all we have left. To them, though? We're nothing but a body in a seat or a weapon to be used. Replaceable. Expendable."

"I can't accept that," Morgan said. She reached for him, but he refused her advance. "Hey. We matter. The work matters."

His eyes seethed with anger. "Keep believing that and your name will be on that wall next to Ruth's. And for what? After what we saw, what we've seen even before Bellbrook. What is really going on out there?"

He turned to leave, but she held him back, fingers locked on his arm. "What happened when you went for help, Lincoln? Zac said you were muttering to yourself as the radio signal came back. What happened?"

Her hand fell away.

"Please. I want to help. I do. I think we both know…"

"Nothing," he answered, his eyes cold and dark. To her, though, they were broken, shattered from the experience. Fear had won and refused to let go for even a second. It frightened her to see him, this strong, resilient figure in her life, brought low by their experience in the now lost town of Bellbrook, Ohio. "Nothing happened to me. Let it go, Morgan. Just like I have."

"I can't. You get that, don't you?"

"Yeah," he said, his voice barely a whisper. "I wish to God I didn't."

He started for the door, and he stopped short next to the wastebasket. He dropped the flowers inside and continued, leaving her with his words, his anger, and most importantly his question.

What is really going on out there?

Morgan sat down on the bench, wishing she held an answer for the spiraling agent of the DSA. There were only more questions and a room full of silence in response.

CHAPTER THIRTY-THREE

Ben's sneakers squeaked along the freshly polished hall of the DSA warehouse. The bright canvas reflected the overhead lights, and the blue laces rested tight along the red-and-white-stripe design. Patriotism came in many forms and he wore his well.

Stephanie looked up from her screen at his arrival and smiled.

"She in?"

"She is." The personal assistant stood and circled the small desk. She leaned close, running her fingers along the twin blood-stains on his tie. She straightened it, fixing the twisted knot at his neck. It pulled taut and fell against his chest. "New kicks?"

"Not exactly the glass Skechers I was hoping for, but what do you think? Am I ready for the ball?"

"Is the ball ready for you might be the better question," she responded with a laugh.

"I've been asking myself the same thing," he said. She opened the door and he stepped inside, tossing her one last grin before she returned to work.

The question stuck with him. His role at the DSA, his place in the world. When this began he'd had a choice to make: to live the life he wanted, or endure a nightmare he didn't deserve. Rather, it was what he believed to be a choice, though it wasn't his own. It was Metcalf's. The DSA or jail was no choice at all, yet it was the only offer on the table. He'd accepted, hoping for a chance to make it work. He'd hoped to figure things out along the way: to find some way to reclaim his former life.

Then Bellbrook happened. The incident had pulled and torn at everything decent about the world. It also gave him something more: a fight—he finally had something to fight for, and more importantly to fight against, in the form of the man behind the loss of seven thousand lives.

Metcalf sighed at his arrival, catching sight of the sneakers clashing against his black suit. "We really need a dress code."

Ben grinned. He took the seat across from her as she removed her reading glasses and set them on the growing pile of reports.

"Personnel files?" he asked, catching sight of résumés among the detritus swarming the tabletop. "Already?"

"No choice," she answered curtly. "Not that I have to explain my actions to you."

Ben nodded. Sleep hadn't come easily to him since their return. Some blame was due to the new apartment at the Edgemont and the lumpy mattress waiting for him. The main issue, however, was his dreams. Ruth had died by his side and there was nothing he could do to save her. There were no words to say. She died and he had been powerless to stop it. The act haunted him and would continue to do so until the man known as the Witness paid for his part in her death.

"You wanted to talk?" Ben inquired. "Is this about Agent Heller?"

"In a way," Metcalf said. "Your report reflects the fact that proximity to the signal accelerated Agent Heller's response?"

"That is my theory. It also explains why Morgan and Lincoln made it out all right."

Metcalf rubbed at her chin, pen to paper in rapid strokes. "Since Agent Dunleavy arrived at the forest after the signal was silenced."

"Correct," Ben said. "Of course, if we had been in Bellbrook longer, who knows how it would have gone."

"Small graces," Metcalf commented, her voice soft.

"How long did Ruth—"

"A little more than two years. Grissom promoted her to the field team after a certain altercation," Metcalf said with a smile. Her fingers grazed her chin. "Still feel that one every once in a while."

"You deserve it?"

"Mr. Riley, I deserve everything that comes my way."

"If we're all set, then?" Ben's hands propped up his body from the cold metal of the chair.

"You omitted one part," Metcalf said. "Your own."

"I'm sorry?"

"Why did he let you live?"

There is a reason you are here. A reason you have been chosen by them.

The nameless individual's words followed Ben everywhere he went. If the Witness knew about his presence at the DSA, if he was aware of his recruitment so quickly, there must have been more to it than a simple set of circumstances. Why had he been chosen out of so many others? The résumés strewn about her desk were evidence that more qualified agents waited for the position.

Ben shook his head. "I'm not sure. Some of what Howard Clevinger mentioned, some of what Morgan believes as well according to her report, but there may have been a secondary trigger. Environmental. Possibly in the water supply or a local food source. Ruth was injured, so it may have been bloodborne. Morgan had a sample, but—"

"Adams took it."

"They were so concerned about our presence, yet they have nothing on the man who triggered all this." The soldiers sent to clean up the forest of Bellbrook had been efficient in their destruction, yet had found no trace of the Witness in their work, since they were so busy removing all evidence of the event from the world.

"About this Witness, as you call him," Metcalf started. "Nothing more coming to you about him? His face? Accent? Features?"

"My reference to Major Toht wasn't enough for you?" Ben asked. He twisted his hand into a claw and reached for the director. "*'Fraulein Ravenwood, let me show you what I am used to.'*"

Metcalf dropped her pen to the notepad to pinch the bridge of her nose.

"No love for *Raiders of the Lost Ark* at all?"

"You're not winning me over."

"He was smart," Ben continued. "Kept his distance. Something tells me he won't for long though."

"Great. So much for sleep in the near future."

Ben agreed. "I did want to discuss the other site."

Metcalf folded her fingers on her desk. "Spring Hill."

"Did Modine find anything?"

"Exactly what you thought," Metcalf replied. She opened her desk drawer and laid out satellite photos atop the growing mass of files. "I had to go through some back channels to get these. No one is answering my requests at the Department of Defense or General Adams' office. Not even to discuss the events in Ohio. Now I know why."

Ben lifted the images of the town. It was the same as Bellbrook in its emptiness. There were no people in the photos, only empty vehicles and empty storefronts. Everything was broken down and forgotten. Ben paused at the sight of the town's outskirts. Fences loomed at all major roadways. Gates barred the path, and army personnel surveyed the grounds outside Spring Hill. Containment. Just like Bellbrook.

"They knew," he muttered. "They knew about Spring Hill the whole time."

"So it would appear. As well as what happened to the residents." Another image shot across the desk. Trees covered the photo—another forest overtaking a school football field. Metcalf pointed at the revelation. "It cropped up overnight."

"Like Bellbrook," he said, his voice lost to the images. "And the public has no clue."

She shook her head. "Chemical spills. Water contamination. I'm not sure how they'll spin this latest incident, but I've been told a story is being put together to explain the whole thing away without anyone getting a decent look."

"At the truth," Ben huffed.

"The truth is what people are told, Ben."

"Forests," Ben snapped. "Forests of people. Just like that. This is what you do? This is what the DSA handles?"

"Today," Metcalf said. "This is what we do today. Tomorrow is another story."

"We should take a look," Ben said. "Call in the CDC. They should have enough pull to make sure we can—"

"No point."

"What?" Ben barked. The door opened behind him. Stephanie peered in to check over the situation. Both Metcalf and Ben waved her off, the latter swallowing hard to calm his nerves. "Of course there is a point, Metcalf."

"Director," she clarified. "And you misunderstand."

She opened the report and another image fell out. Ben lifted it.

"Seriously?"

"I had Zac continue to monitor Spring Hill. This came back last night."

Ben dropped the photo on the desk with the others. The forest was gone, the roots ripped from the earth. Not burned, but taken. Someone was covering their tracks. Maybe the Witness, maybe someone else entirely.

CHAPTER THIRTY-FOUR

Ken Bertram had never seen the CBG Corp. Processing Plant before. He had never even heard of CBG Corp. before pulling into the lot. Trucking was in his past. A mistake had cost him a lucrative career in the industry—one that had taken the life of a man with poor timing in crossing the street.

Odd jobs became the only jobs for Ken. He subbed for different contractors when they needed an extra pair of hands. His wife preferred it. His kids were on the fence. Having Ken home meant life changed for them. His priorities had never meshed with the rest of the family.

When the call came he believed it to be a ruse. Some prank by his old firm, trying to pay him back for the publicity nightmare they'd created in the first place by forcing him to drive sixteen-hour shifts for weeks on end.

It wasn't. The voice, strong and confident, needed people who could keep a secret. The cash promised at the end was too much to ignore. His family held a feast prior to his departure, though it seemed to be more of a celebration at his upcoming absence.

It didn't bother him. Their displeasure at his distance, their inability to understand the shame he felt at his mistake and a decade of silence on the road, made family a difficult concept to fathom let alone stomach on a daily basis.

He met the other seven drivers outside Chicago to pick up the trucks. An overnight trek to Kansas brought them to their destination, and they started back fully loaded. That was when the first deviation arrived. It came in the form of a message passed between drivers and was followed by three more over the course of two days.

Not small detours either. Each one pulled them hundreds of miles from their original destination in South Bend. The drivers followed their individualized routes and changed course, splitting from the caravan that had kept Ken alert and aware of every hazard on the road ahead.

Three days of solitude brought him to CBG Corp. The plant lay in the center of dense foliage, ironic considering what they processed. The other trucks sat in their bays, empty — the task complete. Ken followed suit, his body stiff from the lack of movement over the course of the week.

Ken climbed up to check that the contents remained secure. The trunks of dozens of large trees rested within. The others' trucks had matched his at one point, all from a government site in Spring Hill, Kansas.

Dozens of questions poked to the surface. Ken swallowed them down. Visions of his check kept him satisfied. He whistled a short tune, the song he and his wife had shared at their wedding reception sixteen years earlier. Ken reached for the door to the plant, his bladder waking to the sudden movement. He rushed inside and fell back at the sight of a shadow standing within the frame.

"Whoa there," Ken exclaimed. He removed his ballcap and mopped sweat from the brow. Cold only moments earlier, now his whole body shuddered as if feverish. "Didn't... didn't see you, pal."

The figure remained silent. Ken fought to focus on the man, short and slender, however his eyes wavered. Black dots ran across the edges of his vision.

"Must be dehydrated or something," the driver muttered. He stepped around the figure and into the plant. It was silent within, a rarity considering the constant need for lumber in the world. Ken had never been in a silent plant before. Not even during shutdown. Some background noise always remained, some personnel milling about.

Now only a single sound filled the space. A buzzing, just beyond his hearing. It grew louder with each moment. Ken's hand pressed against his right temple, his left secure against a support beam to stay upright.

"This is a lot of timber for, what did you call it? Research purposes?"

The man circled him in silence. Sweat ran in streams down the truck driver's cheeks.

"Hush-hush stuff, I know. Curious all the same. What do you, um, plan to do with all this?" The dizziness took him and Ken fell to his knees. His hands covered his ears, and his scream was lost to the noise filling his brain.

Then the man crouched beside him, opaque spectacles fastened tight over his eyes and a wide smile across his face. His finger let loose of the red button caught in his grip and Ken could hear again.

"You won't need to worry about that, Mr. Bertram," the man said. His finger clicked the button once more and Ken's screams echoed through the otherwise silent plant. "It will be put to good use. You'll see."

ABOUT THE AUTHOR

Lou Paduano is the author of the Greystone series of urban fantasy adventures, which follow Detective Greg Loren and Soriya Greystone as they hunt myths, monsters, and legends in the city of Portents.

He is also the author of the conspiracy thriller series, The DSA, a serialized tale about a clandestine government agency trying to discover the true power behind humanity's future.

He lives in Grand Island, New York with his wife and three daughters. Sign up for his e-mail list for free content as well as updates on future releases at loupaduano.com.

THE GREYSTONE SAGA

AVAILABLE NOW

Follow the adventures of Soriya Greystone and Detective Greg Loren as they hunt dangerous myths and legends in the city of Portents.

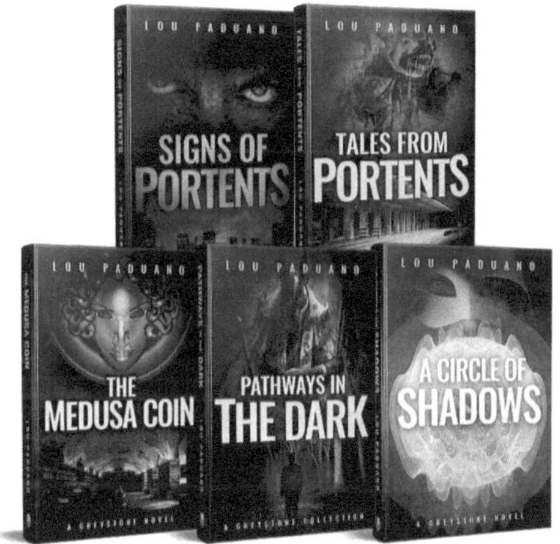

BOOK ONE - SIGNS OF PORTENTS
BOOK TWO - TALES FROM PORTENTS
BOOK THREE - THE MEDUSA COIN
BOOK FOUR - PATHWAYS IN THE DARK
BOOK FIVE - A CIRCLE OF SHADOWS

ALSO AVAILABLE NOW

It's her first case and it might be her last.

Soriya has worked her entire life to become the Greystone—protector of her city, Portents, against the growing shadows of myth and legend. All her efforts are in jeopardy when she is struck down by the destructive power of the Minotaur.

Soriya must now find a new path. Only one thing is certain—she's going to need help.

The secrets of Soriya's training are revealed in the first adventure of this new Greystone trilogy!

THE DSA CONTINUES IN…

What is the Promethean Project?

On the hunt for a lead from the Bellbrook affair, Ben Riley and Morgan Dunleavy discover a dead body and a growing conspiracy. The only clue left behind? A handprint burned into the bone of the victim.

Not everything is what it seems as Connor Hendricks, their FBI liaison, connects this latest death with a series of lab-related arsons.

Caught in a web of lies and illicit drug trials, Ben and Morgan must learn to trust each other or be the next victims of an elusive pyrokinetic.

But is he the killer or merely another victim caught up in a larger game?